"I DON'T KNOW WHAT YOUR GAME PLAN IS, BUT I'M already dirty," he said. "Dirty and dangerous."

Oh, Lordy. Was he ever.

In her haste to get out of his sight, Holly forgot about stepping on his feet. She barely remembered the basket of fruit in her hand.

"No game plan, Mr. Sullivan. I'm merely the Welcome Wagon lady extending you our *warmest* wishes." *Hot* was more like it. Hot, unbridled wishes for things she didn't have, things she would never have with Mr. Benjamin Sullivan, destroyer of dreams.

"Here," she said, shoving the basket in his direction. "I brought you some delicious fruit. Enjoy."

He took not only the basket, but her hand as well. Trapped, with no way out, she stared into eyes as black as the pit of hell . . . and just as dangerous.

"Make no mistake," he said, his voice soft, silky, and seductive. "I plan to."

WHAT ARE *LOVESWEPT* ROMANCES?

They are stories of true romance and touching emotion. We believe those two very important ingredients are constants in our highly sensual and very believable stories in the LOVE-SWEPT line. Our goal is to give you, the reader, stories of consistently high quality that may sometimes make you laugh, sometimes make you cry, but are always fresh and creative and contain many delightful surprises within their pages.

Most romance fans read an enormous number of books. Those they truly love, they keep. Others may be traded with friends and soon forgotten. We hope that each LOVESWEPT romance will be a treasure—a "keeper." We will always try to publish

LOVE STORIES YOU'LL NEVER FORGET
BY AUTHORS YOU'LL ALWAYS REMEMBER

The Editors

NAUGHTY
AND NICE

PEGGY
WEBB

BANTAM BOOKS
NEW YORK · TORONTO · LONDON · SYDNEY · AUCKLAND

NAUGHTY AND NICE

A Bantam Book / December 1996

LOVESWEPT and the wave design are registered trademarks of Bantam Books, a division of Bantam Doubleday Dell Publishing Group, Inc. Registered in U.S. Patent and Trademark Office and elsewhere.

ISBN 0-553-44566-9

Published simultaneously in the United States and Canada

Bantam Books are published by Bantam Books, a division of Bantam Doubleday Dell Publishing Group, Inc. Its trademark, consisting of the words "Bantam Books" and the portrayal of a rooster, is Registered in U.S. Patent and Trademark Office and in other countries. Marca Registrada. Bantam Books, 1540 Broadway, New York, New York 10036.

PRINTED IN THE UNITED STATES OF AMERICA

OPM   0 9 8 7 6 5 4 3 2 1

For Cecilia, my own personal angel

ONE

"Holly, can you come to the office, please?"

Elbow-deep in muffin dough, Holly looked at the clock on the kitchen wall. It was already two in the afternoon. She had three hundred people coming for the Snipes benefit supper, and now she was being called to come to the office.

"Who do they think I am? The miracle worker?"

Although the question was purely rhetorical, Loweva never let an opportunity pass to speak her mind.

"That's exactly who they think you are. If you ask me, this church is named wrong." She paused dramatically and marinated the roast beef before continuing her tirade. "Holy Trinity, my foot. It ought to be called Holy Holly."

Holly laughed. "I thank you . . . and my grandmother thanks you."

"How is the old bird? Mean as ever?"

"Feisty, Loweva. Feisty."

"Hmmph. I've said it a million times—"

"—and I'm sure you're going to say it again."

"—you're too good for your own good."

"Keep that under your hat, and don't forget the green-bean casserole." Holly finished washing her hands, then waved at the woman who was not only the best assistant she'd ever had, but also her good friend and surrogate mother. "Gotta go, Loweva. Keep the ball rolling."

"Hmmph. Without you, there wouldn't be no balls in this church."

Holly was still laughing when she went into the associate pastor's office.

"What's up, Jonathan?"

"Gladys called in with the flu, and I need you to take her place."

Gladys Pipps was the Welcome Wagon lady who went out every Friday without fail, carrying fruit baskets from the church and warm greetings to all the newcomers in the area. Ordinarily Holly would have snapped up the chance to ride around greeting people, but not today, not with so much riding on the success of the supper.

"Can't you get somebody else? You know how important tonight is to the Snipeses."

"There's nobody else, Holly. Grace is making sick calls, and Bob and Jennifer are tied up in meetings. The rest of the staff are off at the youth retreat."

"Margaret?"

"I can't spare her. We've got to get the bulletin out today. . . . You're all I've got, Holly."

Sometimes Holly wished she were two people. It would help, though, if she didn't *look* like two.

"All right. Give me the list."

"There's only one newcomer. That's why I thought you could handle it with no trouble."

"Great." Holly looked at the name. Benjamin G. Sullivan III. She was primed to say, *Wonder what the G stands for?* when she saw the address. 2314 Mockingbird Lane. It was an address that she knew well. Holly used to go there in the evenings when her work was done and sit on the front porch to hear the whippoorwills calling to each other through the dusk.

"No way." She slammed the list onto Jonathan's desk. "There is no way I'm going out there and welcome the man who stole the Snipes farm."

"Now, Holly . . . he didn't steal it. He merely bought it."

"Yeah . . . for a song, and he's singing it himself. I'm not going to do it, Jonathan."

Jonathan tapped his teeth with his pencil eraser, an act that boded ill for Holly. She knew even before he said anything that she had no choice.

"I don't want to go so far as to say that you *have to*, Holly."

"All right . . . all right." She snatched up paper. Not that she needed it. The Snipes farm had been a second home to her. She could find her way there in the dark. "Where's that blasted fruit basket?"

"Right behind you, on that credenza . . . and, Holly, smile when you deliver it to Mr. Sullivan."

She stretched her mouth into a grimace that showed all her teeth. "I'm smiling. See?"

Her ponytail looked like a Brillo pad sitting on the back of her head, and her sweatshirt had a stain on the front where juice from the roast beef had spattered, but she wasn't about to spiffy up for the likes of Benjamin Sullivan. She didn't cotton to thieves.

As she stalked to the car the fruit basket banged against her thighs. Probably making black-and-blue marks.

To top it all off, her car wouldn't start. She stalked back to the kitchen.

"Loweva, can I borrow your car?"

"Lordy mercy! Who you fixing to kill?"

"Do I look that bad?"

"Worse, you look like you've already committed murder and are fixing to add mayhem to the list."

"That's not such a bad idea. . . . Hand me a bag, Loweva. If anybody deserves this fruit, it's the Snipeses." Holly dumped the contents of the fruit basket and rummaged in the bottom of the refrigerator for substitutes.

"What you fixing to do with all them old oranges? They've already gone mushy."

"I'm hoping for worse."

Suddenly Loweva grinned. "Gladys is sick, and you're taking rotten fruit on the Welcome Wagon. Lordy, I can't wait to hear what all else you fixing to do."

Holly's mind began to whirl with possibilities. Maybe this trip was going to be worthwhile after all.

"Bye, Loweva. Wish me luck."

"I figure it's whoever is getting that rotten fruit that needs all the luck."

If anybody had been riding along with Holly in Loweva's 1988 white Cadillac, they'd have seen a rather angelic-looking woman singing "White Christmas" right along with Bing Crosby on the radio. What they didn't see was the wheels turning in her mind.

Holly almost lost her resolve when she came to 2314 Mockingbird Lane, an exalted name for a lowly dirt road with ruts so deep that once she thought the big Cadillac was going to get stuck in a mud hole caused by recent downpours. Other parts of the world might be a winter wonderland in December, but Mississippi in the last month of the year is usually wet and soggy and too cold for a sweater but not quite cold enough for a winter coat.

Holly's tires spun in the ruts, slinging mud every which way. Now she would have to spend six dollars to have Loweva's white car washed.

"You'll pay for this, too, Mr. Benjamin Sullivan the Highfalutin' Third."

Holly parked underneath a magnolia tree, and got mud all over her hands when she got out. She didn't bother to wipe it off. Being covered with dirt seemed appropriate for the task at hand.

She climbed the front-porch steps, being careful of the third one, which had cracked when little Timmy Snipes tried to sneak his pet donkey into the house. Now Timmy and his family were living in two cramped rooms with Michael Snipes's sister, and the pet donkey was out in the pasture looking lost and forlorn.

Ignoring the bell, which was still broken unless the thief had fixed it, Holly pounded on the front door. If the door hadn't been so hard, she'd have banged louder. It was a good way to let off steam.

The soon-to-be recipient of the rotten fruit was not home, but women bent on revenge don't give up easily. Holly stalked around the house, looking for her target.

There he was, sticking out from under Michael Snipes's tractor. At least part of him was, a good-looking part—the finest pair of legs she'd ever seen outside slick magazine ads for suntan oil and fun in the Bahamas.

She hoped and prayed that this was not Benjamin Sullivan, and that if it was, the hidden part of him didn't look as good as the parts she could see.

"Benjamin Sullivan?" she said.

For a moment he was perfectly still, and then the legs began to move in her direction. They were followed by a torso that was the stuff of dreams—trim hips, flat belly, and a fine waist widening to a pair of shoulders that would have made her swoon if she hadn't known they belonged to a scoundrel.

"Oh, Lord," she said, but she wasn't praying, except maybe for herself.

The face that emerged was smudged with grease, but it could have been covered with mud and still send women fainting in the aisles. Dark hair tumbled toward a pair of arched eyebrows and eyes so bright and black they looked like the jet beads in her grandmother's jewelry box.

He lay on the ground for a small eternity simply staring up at her.

He couldn't have put her more at a disadvantage if he had tried. Women over thirty should never be viewed upside down, especially women who carried a tad too much extra weight. Well, more than a tad, actually, but Holly had too much else on her mind to think about that right now. Upside down was an unflattering angle, guaranteed to make the bags under her eyes look like bulging suitcases, to make her thighs look like tree trunks, and to uncover the multitude of sins the loose sweatshirt was meant to hide.

With any other man she would have gotten through the embarrassment of this first meeting by pretending that she was tall and skinny and had just won the Publisher's Clearing House Sweepstakes. But this was not *any other man.*

"You *are* Benjamin Sullivan, aren't you?" she said, hoping—no, praying—that he was not.

"Yes, I'm Ben Sullivan. Who wants to know?"

It advanced her cause that he wasn't polite. She stepped closer to him, close enough to tromp down on his hand. Hard.

"Excuse me," she said sweetly. "Sorry," she added, not sorry at all. For once she was glad for the extra pounds. Under the guise of shifting her position, she bore down on his hand, all one hundred and fifty pounds of her.

"Oh, dear me," she said, "I *do* apologize. Did I hurt you?"

"No," he said. She tried not to show her disappointment. "Sorry," he added.

It was then that she knew she was dealing with a dangerous opponent.

The way he moved was just like the rest of him, sexy and gorgeous. He towered over her, six-four if he was an inch, and every inch of him delicious looking.

Run, her instincts screamed, but she wasn't finished with him yet. Not by a long shot.

"And you are . . . ?" He left the question hanging.

"The Welcome Wagon lady," she said, momentarily distracted as the wind ruffled his dark hair. He looked like something you'd want to set up on a shelf and flank with lighted candles . . . if you didn't know what a rotten skunk he was.

"The Welcome Wagon lady?" Did he step in closer, or was it her imagination?

"Well, not exactly. A substitute lady, actually."

"A substitute lady?" His black eyes gleamed with mischief, and he boldly stepped closer, this time leaving no doubt.

Her heart was pounding as if she'd run all the way

from Holy Trinity to Mockingbird Lane, and she was beginning to sweat. She wished he would move back a tad, say all the way into the next county.

She drew a deep breath, sucked in her stomach, and tried to regain control of the situation.

"Are you sure I didn't hurt you?" she asked with such saccharine sweetness that she nearly made her own self gag.

"I'm immune," he said.

To hurt or to her? She didn't know, and he wasn't giving away a thing.

It was not at all the kind of answer Holly wanted or expected. Besides that, he was so close, she could feel his body heat. And what it made her want to do was definitely not what a woman in her right mind would ever do with an enemy.

If she didn't do something fast, she was in trouble. Holly did the first thing that came into her mind. Reaching up, she patted the front of his shirt.

"Well, now, isn't that—" She stopped dead in mid-sentence.

Enough electricity to keep a good-size city up and running during a three-week blackout jolted through her. What she had meant to say was *nice*. What she had meant to do was transfer the mud from her hands to his shirt. What she did was stand there like a fool and savor the feel of the magnificent, rock-hard chest underneath his shirt.

He caught her wrists in an iron grip and held them for so long that she actually shivered. Was it

fear? Excitement? Rage? At this point Holly was beyond knowing . . . almost beyond caring.

"I don't know what your game plan is, but I'm
already dirty," he said. "Dirty and dangerous."

Oh, Lordy. Was he ever.

In her haste to get out of his sight, Holly forgot
about stepping on his feet. She barely remembered
the basket of fruit in her hand.

"No game plan, Mr. Sullivan. I'm merely the
Welcome Wagon lady extending you our *warmest*
wishes." *Hot* was more like it. Hot, unbridled wishes
for things she didn't have, things she would never
have with Mr. Benjamin Sullivan, destroyer of
dreams.

"Here," she said, shoving the basket in his direction. "I brought you some delicious fruit. Enjoy."

He took not only the basket, but her hand as well.
Trapped, with no way out, she stared into eyes as
black as the pit of hell . . . and just as dangerous.

"Make no mistake," he said, his voice soft, silky,
and seductive. "I plan to. I plan to enjoy every bit of
this to the hilt."

He released her with such suddenness that she
almost lost her balance.

As if that weren't enough, it started to rain. Water
soaked through her sweater and drenched her hair.
She felt like a soggy mass of dough.

She left him without saying good-bye, left him
standing there with a basket of rotten fruit in his hand
and a smile on his lips that didn't bode well, especially
for her.

What was he thinking as she walked away?

Don't be a fool, she told herself. Men like him only thought about women with bleached-blond hair who could eat six doughnuts without gaining an ounce.

As if she needed anything else to go wrong, her shoelaces had worked loose and were dragging in the mud. Trip or tie? That was the question. She opted to bend over and tie the troublesome things.

Some sixth sense made her sneak a peek in the direction of Ben Sullivan, and there he was, bold as brass, making no bones about viewing her from behind—which was a thousand times worse than viewing her upside down.

"Oh, Lord, why did I have that second helping of lasagna last night?" she said.

She gave him a jaunty little wave and a brave smile, then hastened to her car and sat there mortified, a short fat mushroom who longed to be a svelte stalk of celery.

"Shoot," she said, striking the steering wheel. Even her dreams of being thin involved images of food. In spite of the indignity of being viewed from behind, she cranked her borrowed car and drove off like a real lady.

"At least I'm in a Cadillac," she said . . . as if Ben Sullivan would have cared if she had been on a rocket ship full of Twinkies.

TWO

Ben Sullivan stood in the rain watching until the white Cadillac had disappeared down the lane. Then he plucked one of the oranges out of the basket. Its sides caved in, and juice ran over his hand, not the sweet sticky juice of a delicious ripe orange, but the tart-smelling juice of an orange long past its prime.

Suddenly Ben roared with laughter. He laughed so hard, tears ran down his face.

Still laughing, he selected another orange. It was in even worse condition than the first, disintegrating the minute he touched it.

Suddenly Ben became thoughtful. A man in his position had many enemies. Which one of them hated him so much that they would send an impish red-haired dynamo to trample his hand, smear mud all over his shirt, and deliver a basket of overripe oranges?

Maybe there was worse at the bottom of the basket. Cautiously he searched. Nothing there but fruit.

He was being paranoid, of course. Living all those years in D.C. could do that to a man. Dirty deals and dirty politicians. Fast cars and fast women. The only wagons were the paddy wagons, taking in the drunkards, the thieves, and the prostitutes . . . those that hadn't found the cushy beds of some high-powered protector.

It was a city that stole a man's soul. That's why Benjamin had left . . . to see if he still had a soul.

Chance had brought him to Mississippi, chance and a good real-estate agent.

"I've got the perfect place for you, Ben," Wayne Fiorelli had told him. "It needs a little work, but you can pick it up for a song and sing it yourself."

The place was exactly what Ben wanted, not ramshackle but needing enough attention so that he could be as busy as he wanted to be while turning it into something that was his.

So, get to work, he told himself, instead of standing in the rain like a fool. There were boxes to be unpacked, doors to be properly hinged, front steps to repair . . . a thousand chores that begged for his attention.

Hines was back, standing in the kitchen in his suit and tie, holding two bags of groceries. His eyes swept over Ben, taking in the wet head, the muddy shirt, the hand that was beginning to turn black-and-blue.

"Good grief, sir. What happened to you?"

No matter how many times Ben said that he didn't want to be addressed as *sir*, Hines persisted.

"I was born in Virginia, sir," he would always say, as if that were explanation enough.

A slight dapper man of fifty, Nathan Beauregard Hines was of the old school—hardworking, dedicated, loyal, and respectful toward his elders and toward his employer. He had served as Ben's man Friday for ten years, and when Ben made the move to Mississippi, Hines had moved too.

"I can help you find suitable employment in D.C.," Ben had told him. "There are many people here who could use a man of your talent."

"I wouldn't dream of letting you go off to the wilderness by yourself, sir."

"A farm in Mississippi is not the wilderness."

"Anyplace without a convenience store on the corner is the wilderness."

Hines had never wavered in his opinion, even after discovering that a convenience store was located a mere ten minutes from the farm.

Ben plucked one of the bags from him. "I tangled with the Welcome Wagon lady."

"The Welcome Wagon lady?"

"The hate wagon lady might be a more appropriate name," Ben said, grinning. "Man, she had a fire under her tail that wouldn't quit. A nice tail, too, by the way."

"And of course you noticed."

"I'm not dead, am I, Hines?"

"I don't know, sir. Sometimes I wonder."

One of Hines's fondest dreams was to see Ben married with kids.

"You have so much to offer, sir," Hines said. "A handsome, successful man like you should have a wife and children. It's a sin."

Ben had seen sin. Sin was a marriage of mortal combat, like the one his parents had. Sin, D.C. variety, was marriage to one woman and sleeping with six. Sin was fathering children then abandoning them to the care of irresponsible nannies and tutors and baby-sitters.

He was a confirmed bachelor by choice. Nothing was going to change that. Still, from time to time Hines tried.

"If this is going to be the short version of your lecture on the joys of marriage, I'll stay and help unpack groceries. If it's going to be the long one, I'm leaving. . . ." Hines grunted at Ben's words. "By the way, I'll bet you were the only one in the grocery store wearing a suit and tie."

"Be that as it may, I would look ridiculous in some of those costumes these people call clothes."

Ben chuckled. Though there was not much for a man of Hines's considerable organizational and business skills to do on the farm, Ben was glad he had come. Solitude would not have been bad, but loneliness could be brutal.

Inside the kitchen the two men worked in comradely silence, the only sounds the rattling of paper bags and the slamming of cabinet doors. Suddenly there was a new sound, a loud and raucous braying.

"Did you say something, Hines?"

Hines walked to the window, then came back to report. "If I'm not mistaken, there's a jackass out there in the back forty who requires your attention."

"I thought I left all of them up in D.C."

Hines grinned at him. "Sorry to disappoint you, sir."

"You might want to loosen your tie before you go out there and see what he wants."

"I daresay he wants feeding. I'm sure you'll figure it out, sir."

"If I don't do any better with him than I did figuring out the tractor, we're all in for a tough winter."

"One of the many joys of being a farmer, I hear."

Ben found the donkey's feed in the barn, right where the former owners had said it would be.

"Piece of cake," he said, but the donkey would have nothing to do with him or with the feed bucket.

Ben had taken over the farm—lock, stock, and barrel. The transfer of ownership had been done so hastily that he hadn't even had time for a crash course in farming. Not that he intended to raise crops, but he did fancy the idea of owning farm animals. There was something extraordinarily peaceful about sitting in a front porch swing and watching cows and sheep graze and donkeys do whatever donkeys did.

Ben cajoled and begged, but the donkey merely watched him with a jaundiced eye.

"All right. Have it your way." Ben set the feed

bucket inside the open stable door. "If you change your mind, the food is in here."

Back at the house, Hines had turned his attention to the fruit basket.

"Sir . . . what do you want me to do with this?" He held the object as if it were a vial of deadly virus.

"Just toss it." Suddenly Ben remembered the stubborn tilt of a chin, the blue eyes shooting fire. He didn't even know her name. "Wait."

He retrieved the brochure from the bottom of the basket. HOLY TRINITY CHURCH was printed in bold letters across the top. Then a color photo of the church and grounds, followed by a list of the church personnel, the pastors and staff. Grace, Gladys, Jennifer, Holly, Margaret. Which one was she?

He hadn't set foot in a church in years, and he wasn't about to go to church just to find out the name of a woman who had bruised his hand and smeared him with mud.

He was about to toss the brochure into the wastebasket when another list caught his eye.

Activities, the heading said. The first thing on the list was a benefit supper. It didn't list the charity, but that didn't matter.

"Does the car have plenty of gas?"

"Nearly full. Are you going out, sir?"

"Yes . . . to a church supper." His expression dared Hines to comment. "A man has to eat, doesn't he?"

THREE

Holly saw Ben Sullivan the minute he walked in. Who could miss him? Six feet of gorgeous male. Two yards of pure unadulterated sex appeal. Seventy-two inches of wicked temptation.

"Holly, where do you want me to set this collection box? *Holly!*"

Loweva was talking to her, but Holly couldn't have cared less about what she was saying. Ben's black eyes swept the room as if he were looking for something—or someone. Could she be the one? Could . . .

Oh, Lordy. She was in costume. Her idea had been to look like a Christmas angel, but Loweva had thrown up her hands when Holly walked in.

"Am I that bad?" Holly said.

"You look like somebody draped you in a bedsheet and threw tinsel at you."

"I don't look like an angel?"

"Not so's you'd notice."

Would Ben notice? Not if she moved fast. Just as she started toward the kitchen he caught sight of her. There was no mistaking his look of wicked glee.

"Well, shoot," Holly said.

"If I had a gun, I would," Loweva drawled. "I smell trouble . . . and it's coming from that hunk over by the door. Who is he anyhow?"

The question brought Holly to her senses. How dare he, of all people, show up tonight? If he had come to gloat, he had come to the wrong place.

"Mr. Benjamin G. Sullivan, the Third." She pronounced each syllable as if she were spitting nails. "New owner of Michael and Jo Ann Snipes's farm."

"Well, if that's not gall, I don't know what is. . . . What are you going to do about this turn of events, Holly?" Loweva asked.

What was she going to do? She could think of about a dozen things, all of them totally inappropriate for the fellowship hall of a large and respectable church.

"Hand me that donation box," she said.

"You're not fixing to ask *him*?"

"Watch me."

"Lordy, Lordy," Loweva muttered. "All hell's fixing to break loose. And in the church to boot. If that man's got a lick of sense, he'll turn tail and run."

Bedsheet billowing, Holly bore down on the enemy like a steamroller headed for a hapless patch of wild oats, an angel of mercy transformed to an angel of vengeance. She figured the costume gave her an advantage. No woman in her right mind would wear such unflattering garb in public. That ought to give Mr. Benjamin Sullivan pause. There was no way to win against a woman with nothing to lose.

"Good evening, Mr. Sullivan." She gave him a big false smile that showed every one of her teeth. "I see you accepted my kind invitation to dinner."

Mirth lit his face. "You were being kind . . . ? I pity the poor soul who feels your ire."

"Why, thank you, Mr. Sullivan."

"Don't thank me. I haven't done anything." His black eyes swept over her, pausing at the folds of white over her breast and lingering at the tinsel halo, rakishly askew on her flaming red hair. "Yet," he added.

Oh, Lordy, what a man's voice could do a woman's resolve. And his eyes! She got goose bumps thinking of all the things a man's eyes could promise.

Tightening her hold on the pasteboard box. Holly tried to work herself back into a righteous frenzy. With Ben Sullivan so close, all she succeeded in doing was working herself into a sweat wondering what his chest would look like naked.

Traitor, she chided herself. She would have to do better than that.

"No, but you're going to," she said, a cat hiding her sharp teeth and claws behind a soft purr.

He quirked an eyebrow. It gave him a rakish look that reminded her all too well of Max and Bill, her ex-husbands. Both had been handsome devils, devil being the operative term.

She had spent her time in hell, thank you very much. She had no intention of taking that trip again, no matter how much Mr. Benjamin Devil Sullivan tempted her.

"It will be my pleasure . . ." he said, "and yours."

Lord, men like him ought to be declared armed and dangerous, she thought. They ought to be banned from the company of women, especially red-headed angels.

The wicked smile she gave him would have been warning enough for the people who knew her. Unfortunately for him, he didn't know her. And she would see to it that he never did.

"Oh, but you're wrong," she said. "The pleasure will be all mine."

"As intriguing as it is to pursue this philosophical discussion on the nature of pleasure"—he paused—"let's get down to basics first."

Holly felt hot all over. Ben Sullivan had a way of making the most mundane conversations seem racy and exciting. She had a sudden vision of the two of them getting down to basics—male and female, alone in the garden without even a fig leaf. She wet her dry lips with the tip of her tongue.

Ben never took his eyes off that tiny tip of pink. Holly figured her heaving bosom was enough to give angels everywhere a bad reputation.

"By all means," she said, noticing with alarm that she was losing some of her steam. If she didn't get this over with soon, Loweva was going to have to mop her off the floor. Her knees had already turned to butter, and her insides were nearing the point of meltdown.

What was the daring Mr. Sullivan going to say next? Surely something entirely too wicked for the ears of Jill and Fred Cramer, who were standing in the buffet line waiting for a big chunk of roast beef. They were listening too. Holly could tell by the angle of their heads and the way their own conversation hushed when she or Ben spoke. That was the downside of being a part of a small community: Everybody made Holly's business their own. Usually the motive was not malicious. The good people of her church merely wanted to make sure that she was coming to no harm.

Discretion being the better part of valor, Holly decided to move her discussion with Ben into the safety of the empty hallway.

Ben looked pointedly at the hand she put on his arm.

"What's the weapon this time?" he said. "Mustard? Catsup?"

"Why, Mr. Sullivan. How you *do* misinterpret my motives."

Grinning, he shook his head. "I was going to ask your name, but I see I'm in the company of none other than Scarlett O'Hara, femme fatale of the Old South."

He didn't need any urging to follow her into the hallway. Two fluorescent bulbs in the overhead fixture had gone bad. Their dim flickering seemed exactly right for diabolical deeds . . . or stolen kisses.

Holly fanned her hot face with her free hand.

"I didn't tell you my name?" she cooed. "Forgive my lack of manners." She had no intention of telling her name. After tonight, he would never have occasion to use it.

He waited for her to speak, then suddenly tired of the game. A fierce and deadly calm came over him. Although he didn't move, Holly had the sensation of smothering, as if he had stepped close enough to pin her to the wall with his magnificent body. She might have called on a Higher Power for help, but she figured God wasn't about to listen to the prayers of one slightly tarnished angel.

When in doubt, pretend: That was her motto. Holly stuck out her chin and looked him straight in the eyes.

"What's your game?" he said. "Or is it merely that you want to be kissed?"

His arm snaked out so fast, she didn't have time to move. At least that's what she told herself while she still had an ounce of rational thought. That, too, vanished, when Ben Sullivan backed her into the wall, his body so close to hers that she was aware of nothing but texture and sensation—rough tweed jacket and crisp wool pants; chest, wide and solid; legs, long and hard. Inch by inch his mouth came closer, so close his hot breath nearly melted her lipstick.

She licked her lips, anticipating his kiss, wanting it so badly, she went weak-kneed and shaky. As if her capitulation weren't bad enough, she was on the verge of making a total fool of herself by moaning.

Ben saved her the humiliation by releasing her so abruptly that she almost lost her balance.

"You *do* want to be kissed."

She covered her flush of excitement by belatedly whipping herself into a rage.

"I do *not*, you arrogant back end of a mule! Especially by the likes of you."

He leaned casually against the drink box. If she hadn't seen his eyes, she might have been fooled into thinking he was relaxed. They were as flat and flinty as a coiled snake's.

"You find me reprehensible, do you?"

"Absolutely. You are the most irresistible—" She might never have known her blunder if he hadn't laughed. "See . . . you've got me so upset, I don't even know what I'm saying."

"I think you know *exactly* what you're saying."

"Ohhh . . . I don't even know why I bothered to speak to you. You're my worst nightmare come true."

She whirled around, intent on making a dramatic exit, but he stopped her with an iron grip on her upper arm. She swatted at him—as if it would do any good.

"Get your hands off me. Is that any way to treat an angel?"

"If you're an angel, I'm a saint . . . and I'm certainly no saint."

"How well I know."

"What else do you know?"

The pressure he put on her arm was just short of

painful. Too late, Holly realized that she had started this fracas. She might as well finish it.

"Enough to make me sick at my stomach," she said.

He probed her with the darkest stare this side of hell. She wondered if he saw what a hypocrite she was, on the one hand hating him and on the other wanting to kiss him.

"I'm waiting," he said.

"For what?"

"Particulars."

"You want particulars? I'll give them to you. Let's start with stealing."

"Stealing?"

"Don't play the big innocent with me, Ben Sullivan. At the price you paid for that farm, you might as well have put on a mask and taken it at gunpoint from poor Michael and Jo Ann Snipes."

"The bank foreclosed: I purchased at a fair price."

"You call less than the mortgage fair? Not only do you have their farm, but they're still paying off the difference."

He showed no remorse. In fact, if it hadn't been for the darkening of his eyes, she would have judged him devoid of all emotion.

"I'm a thief." His voice was so cold it nearly made her shiver. "What else?"

"You're a scoundrel."

"I've been called worse."

"See! You can take a little boy's pet without blinking an eye."

"I took a pet?"

"Not just a pet. *Henry*." He didn't bother to ask who Henry was; he just lifted that damnable eyebrow. "The donkey," she said.

"The donkey is nothing but a nuisance. The child is welcome to him."

"The donkey won't leave without Gertrude."

"I suppose you're going to tell me who Gertrude is?" His eyes sparkled with something suspiciously like humor. Was he laughing at her?

"Gertrude is the cow. She and Henry are best friends."

"The Snipes child can have Gertrude too."

"The *Snipes child*? You take a family's home, and you don't even know their names?"

He didn't bother to defend himself. In other circumstances, she might have found that admirable; after all, she was shooting from the hip now, each shot wilder and more unreasonable than the last. But that's the way she was: all or nothing at all. Take the Snipeses, for instance. To most of the people in the church, they were merely a charity case. But to Holly, they were individuals in need of the kind of loving attention she could provide.

"For your information," she said, "the little boy is Timmy, and he doesn't have a place to keep the animals now, thanks to you."

"You give me too much credit," he said.

It was a mild rebuke considering that it came from an unprincipled rogue.

"I'm surprised you had the nerve to show up to-night," she said.

"I take it the benefit is for the Snipes family."

"You take it right."

He raked her from head to toe with piercing eyes, then strode toward the door.

She wanted to say good riddance, but that wouldn't be in keeping with the principles of love and kindness, not that she hadn't already trounced these principles into the mud.

"Too bad you have to leave," she said in a very kind fashion.

"You think I'm leaving?"

He was smiling when he turned around. It was the kind of smile that should strike terror in her heart—if he hadn't already struck so many emotions that there wasn't room for one more.

"You're not?"

"No, I'm not." That smile flashed again. "I haven't had my dinner yet."

Holly could picture it: Ben Sullivan sitting at one of the tables eating her roast beef, too big to blend in with the crowd and too gorgeous to pass unnoticed. How would she ever get through the evening?

"The roast is tough and the muffins are burned," she said.

His hearty roar of laughter filled the hallway.

"One thing you should know about me: I always do what I set out to do, and I came to *eat*."

Eat what? she almost blurted out. Fortunately her

guardian angel was on duty, and she was saved that mortification.

Without another word, he disappeared into the fellowship hall and left her clinging to the donation box and whatever shreds of dignity she had left. It ought to be a sin for an enemy to come wrapped in a package as blatantly sexual as Ben Sullivan.

"Lord, what am I going to do?" she whispered.

Loweva suddenly appeared in the doorway, arms akimbo and mouth pursed.

"No use asking what went on out here, nosirree bob. Any fool can see."

"See what?"

"Women don't get all bright-eyed and flushed unless there's a man done rung their bells."

"Ben Sullivan did not ring my bells." Loweva gave her a look she knew too well. "All right, okay. So what if he did ring a few? I can handle it." Another look from Loweva. "Well, I can."

"How about handling it from the kitchen? Everybody's running around back there like chickens with their heads cut off." Loweva rolled her eyes. "Lord deliver me from volunteers."

Glad to have something familiar to do, Holly swept back into the fellowship hall and straight toward the kitchen, focusing every one of her senses on the task ahead. In spite of all her efforts, she couldn't miss Ben Sullivan sitting at the table between two of the best-looking women in the church, one a blonde so skinny, she had to take tucks in a size two and the other an exotic raven-haired beauty with a body so showy that she wore short shorts to jog even in winter.

"Naturally," Holly fumed, watching them fawn over him. Or was it vice versa? "What did I expect?"

"About what?" Loweva asked.

"Nothing." Holly jerked a pan of rolls out of the oven and almost set her bedsheet on fire. "Shoot!"

She rolled back the flapping sleeves and set about doing her job. The Ben Sullivans of the world probably wouldn't consider it much of a job—social director of a large church—particularly since most of it was done in the kitchen. But Holly loved people, she loved cooking, and she loved entertaining. What better way to combine all three than in the fellowship hall of Holy Trinity?

"Why don't you let me do that before you set yourself on fire?" Loweva took the pan out of her hands. "Whose idea was that angel suit anyhow?"

"Mine."

Loweva rolled her eyes. "I don't know how come I even asked."

"Christmas angel . . . Christmas spirit. I thought it would get everybody in the mood for donating a generous sum to help the Snipeses. . . . I wish we had a bigger crowd."

"You fixing to pass the collection box?"

Holly had a vision of herself winding among the tables with donation box in hand, standing so close to Ben Sullivan that she got drunk on the scent of his woodsy aftershave. There was no way she was going to put herself within touching distance of that man again.

"Loweva, will you—"

Loweva stopped her dead with a speculative look that meant a long-winded lecture would be forthcoming as soon as the kitchen cleared out, a lecture she'd given Holly many times before. Holly called it Loweva's "How Come?" tirade. "How come you all the time falling for the wrong man?" was usually the way the lecture started, followed by "How come you let that low-down skunk get the best of you?"

"Never mind," Holly said. "I'll do it myself. Now where did I put it?"

"Here." Loweva plucked the collection box off the cabinet right in front of Holly. "If it had been a snake, it'd have bit you in the tinsel."

The first thing Holly saw when she turned around was Ben Sullivan, a rapt expression on his face. Unfortunately all that rapture was turned in the direction of Miss Size Two. She wanted to hit him over the head with a muffin pan.

Instead, she took a deep breath and smoothed down the sleeves of her bedsheet, but there was nothing she could do about the rest of her appearance, short of a shower, a shampoo—and a six-week stay in an expensive spa. Damp tendrils clung to her neck and her face, and her head was beginning to itch from the tinsel halo. Not to mention that the sheet she wore was a vintage model dating back before permanent press and now looked as if it had come off a bed that had been slept in.

"What you waiting for?" Loweva said. "Christmas?"

"Time to face the music," she said, "and I'm not talking about 'Jingle Bells.' "

She took the microphone at the front of the room. Generally she was comfortable speaking to a group of people, especially this crowd, because they were united by a common purpose, a common cause. But tonight she had butterflies in her stomach . . . and all because of a pair of black eyes that stripped her bare.

"First of all, I want to thank you for coming."

Against her will, her eyes were drawn to Ben Sullivan. He gave her a sardonic smile, and suddenly Holly felt like a hypocrite. If there was one thing she couldn't stand, it was people who pretended to be one thing when they were an entirely different thing. How could she pretend to be the church hostess if her hospitality excluded people she didn't like or understand?

She smiled back at him, a smile of sincere welcome . . . she hoped. Buoyed by her change of attitude, she continued her speech.

"As you know, the purpose of this dinner is to raise money for the Snipes family. If you thought you were getting a free meal, think again."

There was laughter from the audience as Holly held up the box that had DONATIONS printed on all sides in bright red letters.

"Give generously, please," she said.

Somebody in the back of the room yelled, *"Real*

generously. That redheaded angel is liable to come back as the devil if we don't."

Good-natured laughter and kidding followed Holly as she made her circuit of the room, starting on the side opposite Ben Sullivan. She made slow progress because she stopped frequently to chat. One of the joys of her job was being in the company of people she loved, people who loved her in return. In a setting such as the benefit dinner, she often felt as if she were folded in a giant pair of loving arms. It almost made up for the loneliness of her little double bed in her small blue frame house on Robins Street.

She had her grandmother, of course, and her parrot, but both of them were takers instead of givers. Not that she didn't love them. She loved them both and was fiercely protective, but her role was mainly that of caretaker.

It was not the role she had imagined for herself at thirty-three. Long ago she had dreamed of a rambling house with plenty of apple trees for children to climb and lots of space for pets. What would her life be like now if Max hadn't run off with the Tupperware lady and Bill hadn't squandered their nest egg on a red Thunderbird convertible that took him to California and never brought him back?

"No use crying over spilled milk," her grandmother always said. Most of the time Holly didn't. But sometimes, especially during holidays, she'd get close to tears for no reason at all . . . or for reasons she couldn't bear to think about.

"Great meal, Holly. But then, they always are."

"Thanks, Jonathan."

He had brought his entire family, his wife Jean and their four children, all with the smiling blue eyes that made Jonathan so beloved as associate pastor.

"You know Ben Sullivan, of course. . . ."

"Of course," she murmured, not daring to look.

"I've been telling him what a wonderful job you do here at Trinity."

"He thinks your halo is real," Ben said.

Ben winked when she turned to face him, but it was the wicked gleam in his eyes that almost undid her.

Holly was struck speechless, but Miss Size Two and the Body quickly filled the gap with inane chatter that he seemed to find fascinating. Why was it that some women were born knowing exactly how to handle men, and some couldn't find their way around a man if they had a road map marked in red and a six-inch-thick instruction book to boot?

Suddenly Holly was eight years old and in the school yard during recess watching her schoolmates get chosen one by one until she was left standing alone. By the time Jim McKay finally said, "Red Rover, Red Rover, send Holly right over," she was crying and in no condition to run.

She was still in no condition to run, but by George, she could walk—and she had no intention of crying.

"Holly . . . wait."

A hand closed over her wrist, a hand that was all too familiar, a strong hand with a sprinkling of dark hair on the top and long, blunt-tipped fingers that looked as if they would know exactly what to do to a woman to make her feel good.

Holly figured that Ben would know what she was thinking the minute their eyes met, but what did that matter? She wasn't out to impress him, and anyhow he was probably accustomed to having every woman he met lust after him. Let him gloat. She could handle it.

What she almost couldn't handle was the confusion she saw in his eyes. A man like Ben Sullivan? Confused? She must be having premature hot flashes. Or maybe she had stayed in the kitchen too long.

The confusion vanished as fast as it had come, and in its place was the arrogance she knew so well.

"You forgot to give me the donation box," he said.

She wanted to give it to him, all right. Smack upside the head. But with an audience looking on, all she could do was smile and pass the box.

She itched to see how much he was giving, but he palmed a bill quickly into the box. She wasn't about to look until she got out of his sight. And she certainly wasn't about to thank him. If it weren't for him, she wouldn't even have to be passing a charity box for the Snipeses.

As she left she heard Jonathan thanking Ben and inviting him to Sunday-morning services.

The irony of the situation struck Holly. With one hand the church did everything in its power to help the Snipeses raise money to pay off their debts, and with the other they reached out to welcome the man responsible for the Snipeses' predicament in the first place.

No wonder Holly had such a hard time walking the straight and narrow. The road to goodness wasn't straight and narrow at all: it was full of dips and detours and unexpected curves.

Holly risked a peek into the donation box. On top of the small pile of money was a five-dollar bill. It had cost her more than that to wash Loweva's car.

The skunk. Did he think that measly little bit would salve his conscience? Or did he even have one?

"Ben, we'd love for you to join us for Sunday-morning worship," Jonathan was saying.

"I'm not a joiner. I don't believe in institutions, any of them."

The sound of Ben's voice raised goose bumps the size of hen eggs on Holly's arms. All of a sudden she wanted to throw away the box, throw away responsibility, throw away principle, and simply wallow at his feet listening to his voice.

And what did that make her?

She was hot and confused, and her head was breaking out in welts from all that tinsel. She reached up and jerked off her halo.

When she got home, Holly was going to have to pray extra hard for grace.

FOUR

"How was church, sir?"

"I didn't go to church. I went to a dinner that happened to be at church."

Hines closed the book of poetry in his lap and studied Ben over the top of his reading glasses. He hadn't seen a black mood like this since they had left D.C.

"Anything wrong, sir?"

"Nothing a good stiff drink won't fix." Ben stalked to the kitchen and rummaged through the cabinets till he found what he wanted. "You want a drink, Hines?" he called.

"Just a small one might be nice."

"We'll have these on the front porch." Ben came through carrying two drinks and a box of crackers.

"Didn't they feed you, sir?"

"I was too damned mad to eat."

Hines sat on the front-porch swing, and Ben

straddled a straight-backed chair he dragged from the den.

"Any particular reason?"

"Yes, but I don't plan to spoil the rest of my evening talking about her."

Hines hid his grin behind the rim of his glass. They drank in companionable silence. Around them the farm was so quiet, they could almost hear each other breathe.

"A pleasant change from all the noise of D.C., isn't it, sir?"

"What?"

"I said, it's nice to be here in this quiet place where a man can hear himself think."

"Thinking is overrated, Hines."

Ben jumped out of his chair and paced the length of the porch. Leaning against the rail, he peered into the darkness. There was nothing to see, not even a shadow.

"I must have been out of my mind," he muttered.

"On the contrary, sir. I think the move will do us both good. We just have to get used to life in the wilderness, that's all."

It was not the move Ben was thinking about, but he didn't tell Hines so. He tossed the rest of his drink into the yard, then picked up his chair and stalked back into the house.

Hines sat on the front-porch swing listening to Ben's noisy search in the den. He drew his sweater close against the chill and took leisurely sips of his drink. The screen door banged, and Ben burst through like something shot out of a cannon.

"Do you know where my car keys are?"

"I think they're in your pocket where you always put them. Are you going out again?"

"I hate to dash your hopes, Hines, but my late-night foray into town has nothing to do with a woman."

"Perish the thought, sir."

"Sarcasm doesn't become you."

"I rather enjoyed it. I might even take it up permanently."

"Not you too . . . I'd say I was being punished for my sins, if I believed in such nonsense. Fortunately, I know better. Pious poppycock, all of it."

When Ben got in the car, he discovered he had forgotten his jacket, but he wasn't about to go back and get it. Call it stiff-necked pride, call it principle, call it any damned thing you wanted to. Just once today Ben wanted to be right, even if it was over a small matter such as driving off into the winter night without a coat.

How cold could it get in Mississippi, anyhow? Besides, he didn't plan to roam the streets; he just wanted to find a late-night show where he could hole up at the back of the theater and forget about a red-headed she-devil who tried to pass herself off as an angel.

"Holly, is that you?"

Her grandmother knew perfectly well it was Holly. Who else would be standing in the middle of the den in a bedraggled bedsheet that made her look like a snowman that had been out in the sun too long? Who else would come in juggling an armload of table decorations and a basket of leftovers? Who else would put up with a parrot who never said a word except *help* . . . and who said it every time Holly came through the front door?

All of a sudden Holly didn't have one more kind and decent thought left in her, couldn't muster one more false smile.

"Who do I look like, Grandma? The Good Humor man?"

"Your brother would never talk to me that way. He's a perfect gentleman."

Her brother was everything she was not—tall, skinny, successful, and married with kids. But if James was so wonderful, why was he never around, not even on holidays? Why wasn't he the one who took Grandma to the doctor or to visit friends? Why was he never the one to go on a midnight search for blankets because Grandma yelled that her feet were cold or her head was freezing, or she was going to die of pneumonia . . . and that it was all Holly's fault?

Holly was tempted to blurt out her frustration, but she held herself in check. James had been six and Holly one when their parents had been killed in a car crash, and Grandma had been both mother and father to them.

Just because she'd had a hard day didn't mean she had to take it out on the woman who had changed her diapers.

"I'm sorry, Grandma. It's been a rough day."

"Hmmph. You should be in my shoes. Nothing but John Wayne on the TV all the live-long day, and him dead and gone. And the music they play on the radio . . . sounds like cats out in the alley wailing." Although Grandma Lily could drive a car when she wanted to and was perfectly capable of walking without assistance, she leaned heavily on a hand-carved cane when she stood up. "Are you going to turn on my blanket so I can go to bed, or do I have to stand here all night with my bad back?"

"Let me get rid of this costume first."

"Well, hurry up. I'm sleepy. That old parrot of yours kept me from getting my nap."

"Popeye was talking?"

"Talking, my hind foot. He was glaring at me with his mean yellow eyes. I don't trust that old bird. If I've told you once I've told you a hundred times, you ought to get rid of him."

Popeye turned a beady eye Grandma Lily's way, then hopped around on his perch so he could face the wall and pout. Holly wanted to wring both their necks.

"Oh, Lordy, I need a break."

She jerked off her bedsheet and tinsel, then pulled on a pair of yellow sweats with matching shirt that asked the burning question HAVE YOU HUGGED A FRIEND TODAY?

"Hurry up, Holly." Grandma Lily called from her bedroom. "If I have to keep standing, I think I'm going to faint."

Holly sighed. All she wanted to do was put her feet up and forget about her day. Instead she raced down the hall, for although Grandma was in good health, you never knew what would happen at her age—as she so often reminded Holly.

After she tucked Lily into bed, Holly settled into her favorite chair to escape with a good book. Unfortunately Popeye came out of his sulk and started yelling for help.

There was a magnet on Holly's refrigerator that read LORD, GIVE ME PATIENCE . . . AND GIVE IT NOW! Usually it made her smile, but tonight nothing was going to help except total escape.

She scrawled a note for Grandma, just in case Lily woke up: *Gone to the movies.*

Holly glanced at her watch. She was going to be late, even for the late show. As she pulled out of her driveway she began to see the humor of her situation.

"Late for the late show. The story of my life."

Six dramas and a comedy were playing, a Steve Martin remake of an old Spencer Tracy film. That was exactly what she needed, laughter and a jumbo box of popcorn.

"Extra butter, please," she said. Nothing soothed frayed nerves like food.

The movie was already playing to an audience of

one, a man who sat in the center of the center row, the best seat in the house, a seat Holly always chose. Should she sit across the aisle just to be polite or sit in the center and leave a discreet seat or two between them?

She stood in the aisle weighing her problem as if world peace depended on the answer. Meanwhile Steve Martin was hamming it up onscreen, and already Holly felt better. Her laughter was full and uninhibited.

What the heck? she thought. She'd sit in the center the way she always did. Laughing and digging into her popcorn at the same time, she made her way down the dark aisle. She was nearly halfway down the center row when the man turned toward her.

"Ben Sullivan," she whispered.

His eyebrow quirked upward. "If you've come to play Welcome Wagon, I'm leaving."

"Put your mind at ease. I don't plan to play anything with you."

"That's a relief." His smile was like quicksilver. "I'm wearing a clean shirt."

"I noticed." She couldn't help but smile back at him. Who could resist? "Is this seat taken?"

"Yes. I have a harem of six women out in the lobby, all fetching popcorn and Coke and candy." He flashed that smile again, the one that made her forget about her buttered popcorn. "You don't have to sit so far away. I won't bite."

Vivid images of Ben Sullivan biting her neck and other erogenous zones made Holly suck in a sharp breath. She was grateful for the darkness that hid her blush.

"Is that a promise?" she said.

His eyes glowed in the faint light from the movie screen as they raked over the front of her shirt, taking in the slogan and everything that lay underneath.

"Only for tonight," he said.

In the daylight he was sexy; in the darkness he was pure dynamite. She sat one seat down from him and tried to concentrate on the movie, but all she could think of was the large dark shadow that loomed beside her, stealing her breath.

"Have you, Holly?"

His voice came out of the darkness, soft and sexy. How could she hate a man who sounded like that?

"Have I what?"

"Hugged a friend today?"

"Yes. Lots of them."

He turned back to the screen, and Holly dug into her popcorn. Somehow it had lost its savor.

"How many?" he said.

"How many, what?"

"Friends."

She took a swift mental count before answering. "At least ten."

"You have *ten* people you like well enough to hug?"

"Well . . . yes. More, actually. I like people."

"Present company excepted, of course."

There was a subtle tingling somewhere inside

Holly as all her notions of good versus bad, love versus hate shattered like broken crystal.

"I don't *dislike* you . . . I just don't like what you did."

He turned the full force of a sardonic smile on her. "On Capitol Hill we call that doublespeak. Some call it worse."

"Oh, dear." In the course of one short day Holly had come to see herself as hypocrite and now as a liar. Instead of asking for grace, she was going to have to pray for a complete overhaul. To atone, she held her box toward Ben.

"Would you like some popcorn?"

"Is that a trick question? I say yes, and you dump it into my lap?"

She looked so aggrieved that he laughed.

"I was just trying to be nice." She jerked the box back.

"Wait . . ." He caught her wrist. "Does it have butter?"

"Lots . . . I always ask for extra."

If he'd said *I can see that you do*, she would have slapped him.

"I'll lick your fingers if you'll lick mine," he said.

"Oh . . ." Her face was so hot that he would surely see. "You . . . you're . . ."

"An ass, I think is the word you're looking for." He clipped the box out of her hand and dug into the popcorn. When he handed it back, his hand lingered over hers. "That is an intriguing idea, though, isn't it?"

Mesmerizing was more appropriate. It was several long seconds before Holly recovered enough to reply.

"I don't know what to say to you . . . some fast-talking Yankee from Washington. You must be a politician."

"No. Worse. A lobbyist."

He stared at her in the half-light from the movie screen, his face full of fierce challenge. She wasn't about to comment on his profession. All she knew about lobbyists was what she had heard—none of it good.

That was just her luck—falling for the wrong kind of man. Not that she was falling, of course, maybe just slipping and sliding a little. Nothing serious. Nothing that couldn't be corrected if she put her mind to it. Wishing she had sat anywhere except in the center row, she pulled back into the corner of her seat as far away from him as she could get.

Suddenly he was out of his seat and into the one next to her, his broad shoulders and his left leg brushing intimately against hers.

"This makes more sense if we're going to share the same box of popcorn."

Oh, Lordy, she couldn't breathe, let alone reply. Her hand shook as she passed him the corn.

"Are you afraid of me, Holly?"

If he had spoken the question with arrogance, she'd have marched out of the theater and never looked back. But there was an underlying wistfulness that gave her pause.

"No," she said, not at all sure.

He stared at the screen, full of a dark brooding. She'd never known a man as complex, and if she were smart, she wouldn't try to know him. She was a small-town girl through and through, while he was a powerful man who knew how to make deals with some of the most hated people in the country.

Ben Sullivan was way out of her league. Then why was she sitting there wishing she had the courage to tenderly brush that dark lock of hair back from his forehead? Why was she longing to pull his head down to her breast and stroke his face?

"You should be," he said softly. "Sometimes I even scare the hell out of myself."

He pierced her with a look that sliced straight to her soul. Then, in one of his quicksilver changes of mood, he captured her face between his hands, his eyes full of merry devilment. The swashbuckling rogue was back.

"You have butter," he said.

Oh, Lordy, what if he licked it off? Worse yet, what if she let him?

"Where?" she whispered.

She held her breath as he leaned in close. If he kissed her, she would kiss him back. It was that simple. And that scary. Suddenly he drew back.

"You may be the Welcome Wagon lady from hell, but when you stretch those innocent blue eyes like that, you're all angel. But then, I guess you know that, don't you, Holly Jones?"

"That's what it says on my driver's license. Blue eyes."

That damnable eyebrow arched upward, and the mecurial Ben Sullivan changed to the cynic she loved to hate.

"You ought to take your act on the road. You'd make a million." He pulled a handkerchief out of his pocket and handed it to her.

"Here . . . The butter is on the left side of your mouth," he said, then withdrew into a brooding silence with his face turned resolutely toward the screen.

Grateful for the darkness that hid her flushed face and shaking hands, she wiped her mouth. Now what? Give the handkerchief back and hope he didn't grab her hand?

Hope that he did?

What would Miss Size Two do in a situation like this? Holly knew, for she'd seen the act at church— simper and play the helpless wounded female.

You couldn't pay Holly to play such a role, much as she needed the money. She'd worked too hard for her independence.

On the other hand, there was the Body. All she had to do was stand around looking curvaceous, and men fell at her feet. The only men likely to fall at Holly's feet were the ones she tripped.

Ben's handkerchief smelled faintly of the aftershave he wore. The smell was both comforting and disturbing. Images came to Holly—lazy Saturday mornings in the bathroom, steam covering the mirror, towels wrapped around their waists, the smell of his aftershave and her perfume mingling in a fragrance as intoxicating as love. Christmas mornings before the sun came up, feeling under the warm covers until she found a solid chest, then pressing her face against his naked skin, the scent of his aftershave reminding her of the tree they had decorated together. Summer mornings with the breeze coming through the open window, sheet tangled around their legs, his hands curved over her breast, hers low on his belly, fingers curled in the nest of dark hair, testing to see if there was still life after their night of loving debauchery. His scent on her skin. Hers on him. Glorious smells of intimacy, of security, of love.

"You're crying." Softly, Ben touched a tear that glistened on her cheek.

"Yes." She felt the tears now, wet and salty, running into the edges of her mouth. And then because she was afraid of showing him this weakness, she lied. "I always cry at sad movies."

Too late she realized the movie was a comedy. She waited for one of his biting remarks or that sardonic lifting of his eyebrow, or worse yet, a derisive laugh. But Ben Sullivan did none of those things. Instead he took the handkerchief, cupped her face, and tenderly wiped away her tears.

She held herself perfectly still, not daring to move, hardly daring to breathe. The gesture was as sweet as it was unexpected. Just when she thought she had Ben figured out, he did something that forced her to change her mind. Who was this man, anyhow?

In the faint glow from the screen, he looked like a movie star from the early days of film when all the heroes were darkly handsome and dangerously appealing, the days of romance and happily-ever-after when the hero always got the girl then rode off with her into the sunset while some sappy sentimental song played in the background.

Their eyes met, lingered, locked. A tremor went through him, and she felt the aftershocks.

Images flickered on the screen and music filled the theater. On the screen the credits rolled by.

"It's over," she whispered.

He held her a heartbeat longer . . . then two . . . then three. She wet dry lips, and his eyes followed the course of her pink tongue.

"Yes," he said, releasing her abruptly. "It's over."

He was out of his seat and striding down the aisle so fast, she didn't even realize she still had his handkerchief until he was already out the door. And then it was too late to call him back.

"You're always a day late and a dollar short," Grandma Lily often told her.

Sitting in the dark by herself, Holly held Ben's handkerchief to her face, just for a moment, just to be certain the doorman wouldn't see tearstains when she went to her car.

"Hey, Holly," he said when she left the theater. "Did you like the movie?"

There was an enormous decorated tree in the corner of the theater lobby, and flashing silver lights were strung across the exit doors. Holly managed a bright smile by thinking about Christmas.

"It was great," she said, "simply great."

FIVE

Hines was already unpacking boxes when Ben got up.

"Did you enjoy your outing last night, sir?"

"You need to improve your technique, Hines. Any fool can see through that question."

"Oh?"

"You might as well come out and ask where I went and who I saw."

"That's none of my business, sir."

"Precisely." Ben poured two glasses of orange juice and handed one to Hines. "Here. You probably didn't even have breakfast before you started unpacking."

"I thought you might enjoy company for breakfast, sir."

Ben took a long swig of his juice. It was cold and refreshing, and while he drank he thought about what a total jerk he was sometimes. It was not a pretty thought, especially during the season of peace and goodwill.

"By a cruel twist of fate I ended up in the same movie theater as Holly Jones."

"Miss Jones?"

"The hate wagon."

Hines grinned. "Oh, *that* Miss Jones."

"Yeah, *that* Miss Jones."

Ben split English muffins then left them to toast while he got jelly and butter from the refrigerator. A memory assaulted him—a tiny smear of butter on the side of a ripe lush mouth. It scared him how close he had come to kissing her, *really* kissing her.

But the thing that scared him even more was that he *hadn't* kissed her. He was accustomed to taking what he wanted from a woman when he wanted it. Why hadn't he done that with Holly Jones?

"Are you interviewing the butter or do you plan to put it on the muffins, sir?"

Ben looked at the butter in his hand. He was standing with the refrigerator door open like some damned fool. He plopped the butter onto the table and pulled out a chair.

"I don't know why I put up with you, Hines."

"Because you can't do without me, that's why. Would you please pass the jelly, sir? Thank you."

"Oh, it's please and thank you now, is it?"

"Only because I'm planning to include a substantial Christmas bonus when I write my salary check."

"I take it last year's bonus was not substantial enough."

"I plan to add a little for the hardship of living in the wilderness."

"You might surprise yourself and come to enjoy it."

Hines studied him before answering. "You might, too, sir . . . and wouldn't that be nice."

It would be a miracle. Ben couldn't remember enjoying life in a long time. Had he ever? The things he remembered most about his childhood were hiding under the covers with his ears covered so he wouldn't hear his parents screaming at each other, and being shuffled from one expensive summer camp to the next.

In college he'd been too busy achieving to have time for friends. In Washington he had an active social life, but only to the extent that it furthered his ambition.

"Enjoying life has never been on my list of priorities," he said, and if there was a wistful note in his voice, Hines wisely ignored it.

Ben helped himself to the grape jelly. Outside the kitchen window the sun made a bright spectacle of the landscape. It was the kind of day most folks used to lift their spirits. For Ben it was the perfect kind of day to pick out all the flaws on his house so that he could plan how to fix them.

"I thought I would finish the unpacking today, sir, if there's nothing else you want me to do."

"That's fine."

The sun glinted off the wing of a bluebird, and

Ben had a sudden vision of a pair of impossibly blue eyes and a rakish halo set atop a riot of red curls.

"No," he said. "Wait. . . ."

"Is there something else you want me to do?"

Was there? What Ben was about to do would set him on a course that he would see through to the end, come hell or high water. Ben was like that. Ask anyone in D.C.

"Once Ben Sullivan sinks his teeth into a project, he won't quit until it's done," they would say.

"Sir?"

"I want you to find out everything you can about Michael Snipes and his family."

"Is there anything in particular that I should be looking for?"

"I want to know everything, including the kind of toothpaste he uses."

"Consider it done, sir."

That's why Nathan Beauregard Hines was worth his weight in gold. When it came to business, he never questioned Ben's motives. It was a good thing, too, for at the moment Ben hardly knew what they were himself.

They finished breakfast, then Hines left Ben in the kitchen loading dishes into the dishwasher. The brochure for Holy Trinity was still on the cabinet; Holy Trinity where a certain woman who wore sweatshirts advising Ben to hug his friends was probably hatching some diabolical plan to ride him out of Mississippi on a rail.

"Damned fool," he muttered about himself, slinging soap into the dishwasher and slamming the door. For a minute he thought about calling Hines back and saying, *Forget Michael Snipes.*

But that would invite uncomfortable questions, and besides, once Ben was committed, he never turned back.

He headed to the barn to deal with a donkey that didn't like him any better than Holly Jones did. The way his luck had been running lately, the jackass would probably be wearing a saddle blanket giving Ben stupid advice.

He didn't have time to hug friends, even if he'd had them to hug.

Michael Snipes's sister's house was even smaller than Holly's. As she stood on the front porch juggling packages so she could reach the doorbell, she marveled once again that a family of four could squeeze into space that already housed a family of three.

She punched the bell, and Jo Ann Snipes came to the door.

"Holly." Smiling, she opened the door wide, then reached for some of the packages. "Here. Let me help you with those."

Holly followed her into a small room bursting at the seams with furniture. To add to the clutter, winter coats filled the sofa and two opened suitcases took up a good portion of floor space.

"Forgive the mess. We're so crowded. But I

shouldn't complain. Sit down, Holly . . . if you can find a spot."

"Nothing to forgive." Holly shoved the coats aside and deposited gaily wrapped Christmas packages, then held up the wicker basket. "We'd better get this in the fridge."

"Holly, you shouldn't have. You're too generous."

"It's just leftovers from the church supper . . . oh, and some fresh fruit." Holly grinned, remembering how she had come by the fruit.

"The kids will love it."

"They'd like it even more if they knew I took it from the man who stole your farm."

"Holly . . ." Jo Ann's gentle rebuke was offset by her affectionate smile.

"Well, he did," Holly said, no longer sure. Could a man who held her face so tenderly while he wiped her tears be capable of theft? Tenderness and thievery didn't seem to go hand in hand. But then, neither did honesty and political careers.

She sighed. What did she know? She was just a small-town girl who couldn't even figure out two fairly simple ex-husbands, let alone a man as complex as Benjamin G. Sullivan.

"Tell me the story of the forbidden fruit, Holly. And don't look surprised. You always have a story to tell, and you always make me laugh."

Marching around the kitchen using dramatic gestures and making dramatic faces, Holly told about delivering the rotten fruit to Ben Sullivan. By the time she had finished, Jo Ann Snipes was holding her sides.

"Stop . . . stop . . . I can't breathe." She collapsed onto a kitchen chair and fanned her hot face with her apron. "Lord knows, I needed that."

"How is it going, Jo Ann?"

"Not so good. Michael missed another interview yesterday."

Holly's spirits sank. The people in the church had arranged four interviews for Michael Snipes. By now he should have had a job.

"What happened?"

"You know . . . the usual. He overslept, and then the car wouldn't crank." Jo Ann twisted her hands together in her lap. "I don't know, Holly. We can't live with Peg and James forever. Sometimes I wonder where all this is going to end?"

Holly knelt in front of Jo Ann's chair and squeezed her hands.

"I know it will all be over soon. I just *know* it. Hang on, Jo Ann."

"I can, as long as I have friends like you."

Holly felt the press of tears behind her eyes. A fine thing that would be, bawling like a newborn calf when she had come to cheer Jo Ann up. Fortunately, the back door burst open to let in three boisterous, laughing children, and she was too caught up in their excitement to think sad thoughts.

Little Timmy raced forward and grabbed her hand. "Look what Daddy and Aunt Peg got us, Holly. Look!"

It was a Christmas tree of enormous proportions, tall enough to reach the ceiling, with majestic sweeping branches that begged to be decorated.

Margie Snipes caught her other hand. "Can you stay and help us decorate it, please, Holly, *please*?"

She hadn't meant to stay. There was the grocery shopping to do, and then Grandma's bridge game with her friends at Winnifred Griffin's house. Then, the following day was Sunday, an extremely busy day for Holly at the church.

"I'd love to," she said.

And it was the truth. There was nothing like being with children and good friends to make a woman forget that she had no one at home to put the star on top of her own tree.

SIX

"You want me to *what*?"

This was not the kind of news Holly wanted to hear first thing on a Monday morning. She stood in Jonathan's office feeling like a mouse trapped in an enormous maze.

"You're the best one to do it, Holly. You know your way around the farm, you've already made one social call since Ben moved out there, and you know about animals."

The thought of facing Ben Sullivan again on his own turf turned her inside out. He was the enemy, and yet every time she went into battle with him, she lost a little more ground.

"I don't know that much about animals," she said. "Besides, I don't think it's a very good idea."

"The truth is, neither do I. But this is what the children's council voted for, and it's my job to see that it happens." He grinned at her. "That's why I called you."

"Flattery will get you nowhere. You know the man. Shoot, the two of you got along like a house on fire at the benefit dinner. Why can't you go, Jonathan?"

"It's my day to visit the nursing home."

"He'll probably say no." She fervently hoped he would. "What if he says no?"

"It's your job to see that he doesn't. You can do it, Holly. All you have to do is turn on your charm and people walk through flames for you."

"That's twice, Jonathan. You're slipping."

"No. I'm desperate. Look, Holly, I would go tomorrow, but I promised Jean I'd go Christmas shopping. If we don't get this lined up today, we won't have time to make adequate preparations."

"You're going to owe me big time for this, Jonathan."

Holly put off the trip to Mockingbird Lane as long as she could. Not that she had to make excuses. There was enough work in the Fellowship Hall for more than two people. She and Loweva were hanging Christmas greens over the doors.

"Should I call first or just show up on his doorstep?" Holly said.

"You're gonna fall off that ladder if you don't quit turning around ever' two minutes asking me about that man."

"I'm not asking about that man. I'm asking about . . . protocol."

"Protocol, my foot. The last time you got in this kind of stew was when that rascal Jake Farmer promised to take you off waterskiing—and look how all that turned out."

"Snow skiing . . . and it wasn't so bad. . . . I enjoy cooking."

"Hmm, cooking, my great-aunt Astor. You played maid to his high-and-mighty business partners."

"This is not even the same kind of thing. This is church business."

Loweva rolled her eyes. "Like all that *business* with Mr. Sullivan out in the hall?"

Flushed, Holly turned back to her decorating chores.

"This swag needs something. Don't you think it needs a big bow or something?"

"We all need a big *something*, but I'm not fixing to say what."

Holly laughed so hard, she had to get off the ladder to keep from toppling. When her mirth subsided she gave Loweva a quick hug.

"Do you know that you keep me sane?"

"It's a tough job, but somebody's got to do it."

Holly mounted the ladder once more, and Loweva handed up a red bow.

"I'm going to call," Holly said as she tacked the bow to the swag of greenery. "That's the only decent thing, don't you think?"

"Yes, that's what I think."

Holly leaned back to inspect her work. "But maybe it would be better if I just show up. The element of surprise, and all that. What do you think?"

"Sounds like a good plan to me."

"Loweva!" Holly came down from the ladder. "I'm serious about this. What do you *really* think?"

"I think you ought to quit agonizing, then go home and get all powdered and painted up and put on something that makes you feel like dynamite, then go out there and let nature take its course."

"That could be dangerous."

"Honey, I've lived safe and I've lived dangerous, and I can tell you one thing, dangerous is better."

SEVEN

"Do I look like a fool?"

"On the contrary, sir. You cut a handsome figure, but perhaps the tie is a bit too much."

"I knew that." Ben pulled off his tie and stuffed it into his pocket. "I was just checking to see if you're still on your toes."

Repressing his grin, Hines strolled toward the kitchen.

"Where are you going?"

"I have to polish the silver serving tray."

"You're polishing the silver?"

"We can't have Miss Jones taking tea on tarnished silver, now, can we, sir?"

"I call that cowardly, leaving me to face the music by myself."

Hines cocked his head to one side. "Come to think of it, sir, I *do* hear music." His eyes twinkled.

"What do you think it is? Bells in the hills that you never heard ringing?"

"Hines, you've seen too many Broadway musicals."

Ben glanced at his watch. Six minutes after four. Holly was late. She'd said she would be there at four.

In the kitchen Hines was whistling as he polished the silver service. Good grief. The *silver service*.

Did Ben have time to race upstairs and change back into his jeans and sweatshirt, then maybe run down to the barn and find a chore to do? There was always that crazy jackass who wouldn't eat.

He felt like a jackass himself. The way he and Hines were carrying on, Holly Jones was going to think they were excited about her visit. Just the opposite was true. He'd be happy if he never laid eyes on her again. Wouldn't he?

He had started up the stairs to change when the doorbell rang. Hines could get it. As a matter of fact, if he were smart, he'd let Hines handle the whole thing.

"Hines?" he called.

Hines stuck his head around the kitchen door.

"You'll have to get it, sir. My hands are covered with silver polish."

Standing on his front porch with the setting sun as her backdrop, Holly looked like something on a Renoir canvas. The wind had whipped her cheeks to a bright rose, and her hair cascaded over her shoulders like a waterfall of flames. She was wearing an intoxicating fragrance and a soft angora sweater as blue as her eyes.

She looked lush and inviting, and for a moment Ben forgot that contents rarely lived up to their packaging.

"Won't you come in?"

"Thank you."

Ben had always been intrigued by the way women walked, and Holly had it down to an art. Was it calculated on her part, that smooth gliding gait that gave her hips just the right amount of seductive swivel?

When she glanced back over her shoulder and saw him watching her, she blushed. He guessed that was Southern, the ability to blush at will. Whatever it was, it was extremely sexy. And more than a little dangerous. If he weren't careful, he'd find himself believing in the fairy tale people called romance.

Holly sat in his favorite burgundy leather wingback chair and crossed her legs at the ankles. She looked sweet and demure. It helped that he knew she was neither.

"I hope you didn't get the wrong idea about this visit," she said.

"I didn't get any ideas at all," he said.

He'd had years of practice in lying. Funny, though, how hard it was to tell them to this woman in this bucolic setting.

"Oh . . ." Her color deepened, and she pressed her hand over her heart. "I guess I should have told you on the phone. . . . This is church business, of course."

"Of course."

Ben wasn't going to make this easy for her. He stretched his legs out and scooted down in his chair, the picture of repose. It was a pose designed to catch his opponents off guard. He'd won many a battle that way.

"Every year at Christmastime we do something special for the children at Holy Trinity. Last year we did a wonderful little pageant, and they all got to dress up in costumes and be animals. They loved it."

She lifted her chin and dared him to find fault.

"I'm sure they did," he said. "On occasion I enjoy doing that myself."

"Oh . . . my . . ." Holly's eyes widened as she licked her bottom lip.

He almost believed she was real. Almost, but not quite.

Suddenly Ben was mad. He'd sworn he would never be the kind of fool who lost his senses over a woman, and yet here he was dressed fit to kill and sitting idle on a Monday afternoon while Hines plotted to serve tea on a silver platter, and all because of a phone call from the woman who sat in his favorite chair.

"So . . . tell me, Holly, did you come here to ask me to be an animal?"

She shot out of her chair. "You are the most . . ." Her lips trembled as she searched for words to describe him.

"Devious?" he suggested. "Dangerous?"

"I was going to say irritating, perhaps even mad-dening."

If his conscience hurt a little at the way he'd goaded her, he salved it by telling himself that he was saving her a lot of grief in the long run.

"Too bad you can't stay for tea," he said.

Holly gathered her courage. First, she took a deep breath, then she sat back down and crossed her legs at the knee. This was the Holly Jones he knew; assert-ive, focused, certain of herself and her mission.

"If you think I'm leaving, think again," she said, her voice full of a sweetness that he knew was fake. Surprising himself with how much he looked forward to this sparring match, Ben suppressed a grin.

"This could be a long evening."

"Very," she said. "I came for something, and I don't plan to budge until I get it."

"Is that your way of telling me that I have some-thing you want?"

"Yes, but not what you're thinking."

Ben lifted an eyebrow and hot color suffused her cheeks. He held her in a long, piercing look that backfired and sent his own heart racing.

"And what would that be?" he said, his voice a soft, deadly purr.

"You know."

"No, I'm afraid I don't. You're going to have to be specific."

Her eyes widened a fraction, and she moistened her lips with the tip of her tongue. He thought she was getting ready to flee. Good riddance, he would say, but would he really mean it?

For the first time in many years Ben questioned his own motives. Why was he trying so hard to keep Holly Jones at a distance? Was it to protect her or to protect himself? It wasn't a line of thinking he wanted to pursue, particularly with Holly sitting across from him, driving him mad.

Funny how she could do that with a simple look, a small gesture. He'd dated women far more beautiful, far more sophisticated, far more successful and worldly-wise. But none of them had made his heart race. None of them brought out the swashbuckling, protective hero who wanted to take a sword and slay dragons.

Suddenly Ben smiled.

"If you think you can make me leave by laughing at me, think again, Ben Sullivan. I'm not some little wimp who runs at the first sign of trouble. I'm tough, and don't you forget it."

With her jaw stuck out and her lower lip caught between her teeth, she looked like a little girl challenging the school bully.

He left the chair and went to stand beside the fireplace. Propping his elbow on the mantel, he studied her. His den looked better with Holly sitting in it, homier, more inviting, *right* somehow. He was almost sorry that he couldn't keep her there.

But he knew better than to try. He was too smart to fall into that trap.

"You misunderstood me, Holly. I wasn't laughing at you; I was laughing at myself."

"Why?"

"I was sitting there thinking of myself as some kind of hero. Did you know that you have that effect on men?"

"I do?"

"See, that's what I mean. That wide-eyed innocent look. That little-girl blush on your cheeks. It's very appealing, Holly."

"Thank you."

Her smile looked genuine, but he wasn't about to be fooled.

"I'm not sure I meant it as a compliment."

"You think this is an act?"

"Isn't it?"

"I feel sorry for you, Ben. You have all this . . ."

Her sweeping gesture included his leather wing chairs, the antique clock that his grandfather had brought over from Ireland, the fine art collection he had acquired during his world travels, the shelf full of well-loved, well-worn leather-bound books, the rolling pastures outside the window, shadowed with purple now that the sun had vanished.

". . . and yet you're not happy."

Her remark stung. And he certainly didn't want to think of its implications.

"Don't waste your sympathy, Holly. Happiness is overrated."

"I guess that's why you can do what you did."

She didn't elaborate: she didn't have to. The issue

of the farm stood between them like a fire-breathing dragon.

"I never let sentiment interfere with business," he said.

"And I never let business interfere with sentiment."

His smile was lopsided. "They say opposites attract."

"I guess they are wrong."

"Yes. They are definitely wrong."

Once more they were caught up in a long, naked look that said things neither of them dared speak. This time there were no wide eyes and flushed cheeks: Holly regarded him as intently as he regarded her. A log crackled in the fireplace, and a shower of sparks shot upward. The ticking of the clock marked the minutes.

The passion that burst through Ben caught him off guard. At first he could only wonder at its force. Then he had to act. He crossed the space that separated them with long, purposeful strides. His right hand snaked out, caught her chin, and tilted her face upward. Her skin was soft to the touch, and her lips looked ripe and delicious. He leaned down to steal a taste. Just one. And then he would let her go.

She caught a sharp breath, but she didn't pull away from him. Her top lip made a perky cupid's bow, and her bottom lip was rich and full. She was angel and devil and he would have them both.

When his lips were only inches away, Holly spoke.

"I lied," she whispered.

Still holding her chin, still keeping her lips within kissing distance, he quirked his eyebrow.

"You lied?"

"About opposites not attracting. I'm afraid I'm terribly attracted to you."

Her words had the ring of truth. And though Ben suspected it was another act, there was enough doubt to give him pause. He had no intention of giving Holly Jones false impressions. Or any other woman, for that matter. To him a kiss was a casual thing, to be given lightly and taken lightly. He had no intention of making it more.

Regret sliced through him as he gazed down at her. He released her chin, then let his fingers trail lightly down her cheek. When he walked away, his heart was racing.

"Why are you afraid?" he asked, leaning once more on the mantel. The distance helped, but not much. Crazy as it seemed, he still wanted to kiss her. No, more than kiss her: He wanted to ease her onto the Persian rug in front of his fireplace and bury himself in her. He shifted position lest she see the effect she was having on him.

"Because I'm always attracted to the wrong kind of man," she said.

"And we both know that I'm the wrong kind of man."

"Definitely."

"I see. You do this often?"

"Twice. And both of them left me."

"Husbands? Lovers?"

"Husbands."

"It was their loss, Holly."

"You don't have to say that just to be nice."

"Being nice is never one of my motivations. Being honest is . . . sometimes."

"You know, you can be sweet, Ben."

"Don't tell. I don't want to ruin my reputation."

"Actually, I was thinking of putting it on the front of a sweatshirt and wearing it at the senior citizens' breakfast Wednesday." Her grin was spontaneous and impish.

"You have a sweatshirt for every occasion?"

"Not all of them. Particularly not this one."

"What is this one, Holly?"

"Eating crow. After giving you rotten fruit and a hard time, I now have to ask a favor of you."

"So you admit to giving me a hard time?"

"I'm feeling a little bit sorry about stepping on your hand."

"But not about the mud on my shirt . . . and the fruit?"

"Well, no. Actually I think you deserved that."

"Holly Jones, riding around in her white Cadillac serving up justice."

"It's not mine, actually. I borrowed the car from Loweva." He lifted his eyebrow. "My assistant as well as my best friend."

At that moment Hines came through carrying a silver tray loaded with all sorts of goodies.

"Anyone ready for tea?"

Ben made the introductions, then sat back to watch as Holly turned her charm on Hines. One look at his face, and Ben knew that Hines had fallen for her act, hook, line, and sinker.

"This tea is divine, Mr. Hines."

"Just Hines, please."

"What is that flavor? Strawberry?"

"Actually, it's juice right out of a jar of maraschino cherries. I like to experiment."

Hines and Holly were as natural together as ham and redeye gravy. Ben leaned back in his chair and observed. It was fun to watch them, two true Southerners who had never met a stranger.

Her face bright with animation, Holly suddenly turned the full force of her charm on Ben. He wasn't prepared for the impact. He actually felt as if somebody had gut-punched him.

"Now that I have reinforcements, I'm going to get to the point of my visit," she said.

"I can hardly wait to hear," he said, all the while casting around in his mind for a way to prolong her stay.

"I want to borrow some of your animals."

"Ah . . . you *do* want an animal?"

Hines shot him a reproving look. Ben was sure to hear more from him over dinner.

Holly laughed. "Ben Sullivan, you are an incorrigible rake. I take back every nice thing I said about you."

"That's a relief. Sainthood was beginning to bore me."

"Oh, you're far from being a saint," she said. "Very far."

"Would anyone care for a cookie?" Hines said. "They're genuine shortbread, from my grandmother's recipe." He pressed a cookie into Holly's hand. "Actually, Ben is a very fine man. He just likes to pretend that he's not."

"Hines, I don't think Miss Jones needs a character reference."

"On the contrary . . ." She nibbled the edge of her shortbread as she turned to Hines. "I'd like to hear more."

"Not today, Holly." Ben plucked her from her chair like a ripe plum. "If you want an animal, we'd better go down to the barn and pick one out before it gets too dark to see."

"But I haven't even told you what I want them for."

"It doesn't matter, as long as you understand that I'm part of the deal."

"You're part of the deal?"

"Yes. Wherever my animals go, I go."

"But . . ."

"Take it or leave it."

Holly looked toward Hines for support, but he had developed a sudden interest in his tea. If Ben hadn't known him so well, he might not have suspected that he was suppressing a grin.

"I'll take it," Holly said. "Anything for the cause."

Hines was leaning toward them, avidly eavesdropping. Ben steered Holly out the door and out of ear-shot.

"That sounds intriguing," he said. "Anything?"

She swung a glance at him, then quickly turned away.

"Almost," she said. And then: "Why are you laughing?"

"I'm wondering just how far you're willing to take that promise."

EIGHT

It was already too dark to see. The only illumination came from a single floodlight suspended too high on a light pole to do more than transform the fence posts to ghostly shadows.

Then why in the world was she headed to the barn to *see* animals with a man she didn't even trust? Holly knew the answer to that question, and it wasn't pretty. She was out of her mind. Period. Ben Sullivan did that to her, and there wasn't a blessed thing she could do about it.

Except turn around and go to her car. But then he would think she was a coward.

She could thank him politely and say she suddenly remembered that she had someplace to go. But then he would probably ask her where and with whom.

Or perhaps she should—

All thoughts flew out of her mind as Ben caught her hand.

"This path can be treacherous in the dark," he said.

It could be treacherous in the broad daylight with him, but she didn't tell him so. Mainly because she couldn't.

What was it about Ben that turned his merest touch into high-voltage shocks?

The question was silly, of course. It didn't take a Harvard graduate to figure out Ben's assets; they were plentiful and obvious.

The smell of hay didn't help. It was stacked around the barn in fragrant mounds, just right for sinking into and cuddling up with the right man. The bad thing was that Ben Sullivan was the *wrong* man. Holly had to keep reminding herself of that.

"See anything you like?" he asked.

"Oh, yes," she murmured, staring at his magnificent chest. "Most definitely."

"I was talking about the animals." His grin was the most wicked thing this side of Hades.

"So was I."

His roar of laughter startled a pigeon who had taken refuge in the loft. It flapped out into the night, sending a small drift of hay over them.

"You have hay in your hair," Ben said.

She had always loved a man's hands in her hair, and when Ben plucked out the piece of hay, she hardly dared breathe. Suddenly he cupped her face, then slowly, ever so slowly, let his fingers slide backward into her hair. The tingling that started in her scalp spread all the way down to her toes.

"Your hair is beautiful."

She didn't understand him at all. When she was nice, he was naughty. When she was naughty, he was nice. To add to her confusion, his face was naked and vulnerable. She'd never seen him that way. Did she dare trust that she was finally seeing the real Ben Sullivan?

His fingers glided through her hair once more. "So soft and silky . . . it feels alive."

Trembling inside and hoping it didn't show, Holly considered her dilemma. She had never been so tempted by a man, and she was very close to making another terrible mistake.

"I don't know why you brought me out here or why I even agreed to come, but I can tell you one thing, Ben Sullivan, I don't play games, and I'm not planning to fall for any of your tricks—not anymore."

"That's two things."

Even when he was at his most maddening, she still wanted him. The smart thing to do would be to step out of his grasp, but oh, it felt so good to have a man touch her and look at her a certain way. It made her feel pretty and desirable, things she hadn't felt in a long, long time.

In one of his sudden mood swings, he released her and leaned against a support post.

"I can't assure you that my motives were entirely pure, Holly, but I can assure you that nothing will happen that you don't want to happen."

"That's the problem, Ben. In spite of what you've

done and what you are, I'm terribly attracted to you, but I have no intention of being used."

She paused, thinking that he would turn her arguments aside with a remark that was either barbed or witty, but he merely studied her. The look stung her more than accusations. With Ben she had become what she hated most—judgmental and unfair. True, she knew what he had done, but the Snipeses had lost the farm through no fault of his. All he had done was buy it. And she knew absolutely nothing about the man himself except his profession.

"Aren't you going to say something?" she said.

"No. You're having a conversation with yourself, and I'm listening. Carry on."

Holly sank onto an upended bale of hay, then propped her elbows on her knees and her chin in her cupped hands.

"I've tried to learn from my mistakes, and one thing I know is that men like you aren't really interested in women like me."

Except for that questioning eyebrow that shot upward, he was totally impassive. Holly might as well have been baring her soul to a bale of hay. She knew she should stop, but the floodgates were open and the damage was already done. Besides, she never did anything in a small way. With her it had always been all or nothing at all.

"I know I'm no cover girl."

She swung her gaze to him for confirmation . . . or denial. Still he was silent, watching her the way a hawk might observe the animal he'd chosen for dinner. The silence inside the barn was deep and unsettling. Sexual tension was so high, she could feel it, taste it, smell it.

A shaft of moonlight beamed through the rafters and slanted across his face. It wasn't fair that a man with a body to die for also had a face that belonged on a movie screen. She had never felt the contrast between them more acutely.

"I was a fool to come here." She bolted out of her seat. "To think . . . I even dressed for you."

"You dressed for me?"

"You needn't look so pleased. I'll never do it again."

She stalked out of the barn and was halfway up the path before he called to her.

"Holly . . ." Slowly she turned around. "You forgot to tell me where to take the animals."

"I'd like to tell you exactly where to take them, but it wouldn't be nice."

"Are you nice, Holly?"

"Yes. Always . . . except when I'm around scoundrels like you."

In the wink of an eye the nice guy vanished and he became the scoundrel she'd named him.

"Nice can be boring. I'll just have to spend more time with you. Consider it a community service."

"Is that a promise or a threat?"

"What do you think it is, Holly?"

"You don't frighten me, Ben."

"I know, you're tough." He closed the distance

between them and swept her into his arms. "Just how tough are you, Holly Jones?"

Not tough enough to resist his arms, not when they felt like paradise and that was the place she longed to be.

His sweet hot breath fanned her cheek, and his lips were so close, she could almost taste them. Still, she had her pride.

"Tough enough not to let myself be used." She wriggled free, then wrapped her arms around herself at the sudden chill.

"Where you come from kisses may be a dime a dozen, but where I come from we take kisses seriously."

Ben spoiled her dramatic exit by falling into step beside her and taking firm hold of her elbow.

"I don't need any help from you," she said.

"On the contrary, I think you need exactly what I can give you."

"I'm not even going to dignify that remark with an answer."

His chuckle was rich and sexy and made her think of all the wicked things she'd like to do with him under the covers on a cold winter's night.

"Lord, deliver me from men like you."

He opened her car door, then leaned inside before she could slam it in his face. In the glow of the dashboard light he was incredibly delicious, and too much temptation for any woman, especially one who was starving.

"Would you please remove yourself from my car so I can leave?"

He leaned in closer.

"Don't look so alarmed," he said as she backed against the seat. "All I want from you is your undivided attention."

There was devilish mirth in his face, but his eyes were filled with something far more dangerous—a passion so hot and bright, it heated up the inside of her car.

"Mark my words, Holly. When I kiss you, it will be real."

"Would you pass the bread?"

Ben added another slice to his plate then scooted the whole bag of bread across the table to Hines. They worked on their ham-and-cheese sandwiches in silence.

"If you're finished with the cheese, will you pass it this way, sir?"

Ben passed the cheese, then rammed his knife into the mustard jar.

"No need to attack it," Hines said. "It won't bite back."

Ben put his knife on his plate and shoved back his chair.

"All right. Stop this pussyfooting around and just say what's on your mind."

"Is something supposed to be on my mind, sir?"

"You'd never make it as an actor, Hines."

"I wasn't planning to try, sir. I already have a good job." His eyes twinkled. "Unless I'm fired."

"Have you done something I should fire you over?"

"Not lately."

"Not even when you tried to convince Holly Jones of my fine upstanding character?"

"Well, somebody had to do it, sir. You seem determined to portray yourself as something of a scoundrel."

"Maybe that's what I am."

"You are many things, sir, but a scoundrel is not one of them." Hines's penetrating look saw right through him.

"All right. You caught me red-handed. I'm saving her from myself."

"Did it ever occur to you that the lady might not want saving."

"You think so?" A bolt of pure pleasure shot through Ben.

"It appeared that way to me."

Ben was forty-one years old, older than most men when they settled down but not too old to start a family. He had never once thought of settling down . . . until he met Holly. He had never once thought of having children . . . until he met Holly.

Could he be somebody's husband and do it well? Somebody's daddy without turning into his own father?

"I suppose you're going to chastise me for the way I behaved this evening," Ben said.

"No."

"You're not going to tell me what a wonderful woman Holly Jones is and lecture me on missed opportunities?"

"No." Hines grinned. "I don't need to do any of those things, sir. You're doing the job for me, and I must say that I'm delighted by this turn of events."

"There has been no *turn of events*."

"I know what I know."

Ben pulled his chair back to the table, his appetite fully restored.

"Pass the cheese, Hines. And wipe that simpering grin off your face."

"I don't simper, sir. I smirk."

Ben bit into his sandwich with gusto. From a distance came the sound of an owl, and against the window, the rhythmic tapping of a branch blowing in the freshening night breeze.

"You hear that, Hines?" Hines cocked his head. "The sounds of contentment. Mississippi grows on you, doesn't it?"

"Indeed it does, sir."

"I was just thinking, while you're doing that research on the Snipeses, why don't you dig around and see what you can find out about Holly Jones?"

"And what will you be doing, sir?"

"A little research of my own."

NINE

"Are you gonna open that box of candy so's we can have a bite, or are you just gonna let it set there till it gets hard and won't do nobody no good?"

Loweva never lapsed into vernacular unless she was excited. Holly read the card once more to be sure she hadn't been mistaken the first six times.

"Why in the world would Ben Sullivan send me chocolates?" she said.

"What did he say on the card?"

" 'A little something to apologize for my ungallant behavior in the barn.' "

"That sounds like fun. Just how ungallant was he?"

"Wipe that grin off your face. You know good and well what I'm talking about. He's up to something."

"Like what?"

"How should I know? He's a fast-talking Yankee skunk, and I'm not about to be taken in by his sneaky ways. If he thinks he can win me over with a box of candy, he's got another think coming."

Holly stalked to the garbage can and tossed the box in.

"Lordy mercy, have you done lost your mind?" Loweva retrieved the box and wiped it off with a dishcloth. "Throwing out perfectly good chocolates."

"He probably added a little arsenic."

Loweva hooted with laughter. "Just because you delivered rotten fruit don't mean he's gonna poison the candy. If you don't want these, can I have 'em?"

"Godiva chocolates. Can you believe it?"

Loweva untied the ribbon and opened the box. "Now that I can smell it, I can." She passed the box under her nose. "Mmm-mmm, ain't that heaven? You sure you don't want some?"

"Maybe just a little piece."

"Here. It's your candy. You get the first pick."

Resisting the urge to pinch the tops to see which pieces had nuts, Holly selected an oval candy then passed the box back to Loweva. With the candy half-way to her mouth, she paused.

"He wouldn't send chocolates if he thought I was fat, would he?"

"Only a fool would think you're fat, and he didn't look like a fool to me; lots of other things, but not a fool." Loweva finished her chocolate and reached for another. "If I catch him or anybody else even *hinting* you're fat, I'll box their ears."

"What if that's the reason he sent chocolates? That I'm . . . a little plump? What if he sends roses to skinny women?"

"Hush your mouth and eat that chocolate. No sense analyzing all the joy out of something."

"All right. I'll eat it, but that doesn't mean I like it."

The note in Ben's hand was on pink paper with a cutwork border. Holly had even spritzed it with perfume, so that every time he handled the paper Ben got a whiff of roses. To all appearances, it was a prim-and-proper thank-you note. But there was nothing at all proper about its contents.

Dear Benjamin G. Sullivan III, it read.

> You outdid yourself with the big box of Godiva chocolates. I assume they were perfectly harmless since Loweva is not dead yet. Maybe Yankee scoundrels apologize for ungallant behavior in a barn by sending candy, but down here in the South ladies require more: We require a penitent man to grovel at our feet. I'm keeping mine fresh with rosewater in case you decide to pop by and do a little well-deserved groveling.
> P.S. It would be remiss of me not to thank you on Loweva's behalf.

Ben read the note once more and burst into a gale of hearty laughter. Hines folded his *Wall Street Journal*, took off his glasses, and set his paper aside.

"You ought to see this note, Hines. Holly Jones is one saucy woman."

"You wouldn't be interested in any other kind, sir."

"Who said I was interested?"

"You've read the note at least three times."

"Twice. It's damned good entertainment."

"It must be, sir."

"Have I ever received a thank-you note from a woman, Hines?"

"Not that I recall."

"I've sent perfume and roses, I've even sent diamonds, and not once in all these years has any woman ever taken the time to write me a note."

Ben picked up Holly's note and read it once more. Though it wasn't necessarily a thank-you note per se, at least it showed that she was thinking of him, and that was a start.

Ben refolded the note and put it in the secretary. Then he went to stoke the fire.

"She shared with her friend. Did I tell you that?"

"I think you did, sir."

A shower of sparks shot out of the fireplace, and Ben got the whisk broom to sweep them up.

"Hines, would you say a note like that is a sign of class and good breeding?"

"Indeed, I would, sir."

Ben poked the fire once more. "Is there plenty of gas in the car?"

"Yes. Are you going somewhere that I might find interesting?"

"Probably." Ben grinned.

"And what might you be doing when you arrive there, sir?"

"Groveling."

"Lordy have mercy," Loweva said. "Would you look at what just drove up? Wonder who died?"

Holly looked up from the stove, where she was stirring a pot of meatball soup. A white stretch limousine was parked in ostentatious splendor beside the kitchen door.

"Maybe it's somebody coming to the church for a wedding rehearsal," Holly said. "Traveling around in high style is becoming a tradition for Southern brides. Whatever the limo's doing out there, you can bet your bottom dollar it's not for you and me."

"I'll take that bet. How much?"

"*Loweva* . . ."

Holly's gentle rebuke died on her lips, for strolling through the door was Ben Sullivan, primed for mischief in a white shirt that accented his dark good looks and a satisfied smile that said he knew every naughty trick in the book.

For a moment Holly lost her breath, but she made a quick recovery. She wasn't about to let that scoundrel get the best of her.

"Whatever you're selling," she said. "I don't want any."

"You haven't seen my merchandise yet."

If her face was as red-hot as she felt, Loweva and Ben were getting an eyeful.

"I don't need to see your merchandise. I don't like the packaging."

"I consider you too smart to judge the goods by the packaging." Ben halted long enough to smile at Loweva. "It's good to see you, Loweva. How are you this morning?"

"Is this the place where I'm supposed to mumble *tol'able* and shuffle on out of the way?" Loweva's eyes twinkled with devilment.

"I'd be disappointed if you did," Ben said. "Besides, I need a witness."

"For what?" Holly said. "Murder?"

"Groveling."

Holly couldn't have held in her laughter if she had tried. She laughed so hard, she had to wipe the tears of mirth with the corner of her apron.

"Sorry," she said. "I'm all out of rosewater."

"Never mind. I brought my own."

She hadn't noticed the small paper bag in his hand. Ben opened it and pulled out a bottle of rosewater-and-glycerin lotion.

"I'm always prepared," he said, winking.

"Okay." Holly held up her hand. "Enough. I got my comeuppance for that note. You can climb in your limo and leave now. I have work to do."

"It doesn't work that way, Holly. You threw down

the gauntlet, and I picked it up. If you run, you'll disgrace Southern women everywhere, not to mention set the cause of groveling back a decade or two."

Loweva was making no pretense of working. Leaning on the counter, she poured herself a cup of coffee.

"You can't get shows this good on the TV," she said. "Shoot, you two are better than Lucy and Ricky Ricardo. Carry on. I'm all ears."

"Sorry to disappoint you, Loweva, but what I have in mind for Holly requires privacy."

"Hmm-hmmm," Loweva said, grinning. "This gets better and better."

"Whose side are you on?" Holly slammed a lid on her stew pot, jerked off her apron, and used it to shoo Ben out of her way. "Shoo. Scat. Get out of my kitchen."

"I'm not going anywhere without you."

"Do I look as if I've lost my mind? You might charm Loweva with all that posturing, but I know you too well. Wild elephants couldn't get me to set foot in that limousine with you."

Ben merely grinned. "Think you can do without her for a few hours, Loweva?"

"Nobody's indispensable, not even Holly. I can carry on here with one hand tied behind my back."

"I'll remember that treachery, Loweva." Hands on hips, Holly whirled on Ben. "Just because you're the world's sexiest man doesn't mean you can have any woman you want."

His eyes caught and held hers. In one of his lightning transformations, he went from teasing to serious, from lighthearted to intense.

"I only want you," he said.

The promises in his eyes and his voice gave her pause. With all her heart she wanted to believe everything they promised, but did she dare?

No, she decided. Her track record was too poor and the risk was too great.

"I'm not yours for the taking," she said.

They regarded each other in a long silence that hummed with tension. The only sound was the soft clinking of china against china as Loweva set her coffee cup in its saucer.

They were treading on dangerous ground. Holly had felt much safer when they were exchanging barbs. She made herself look elsewhere—the coffeepot, the kitchen clock, the row of copper-bottomed pans—anywhere except into Ben's mesmerizing eyes.

Thankfully, the spell was broken.

"You should be going," she told Ben. "Your limo is waiting."

"It's too bad about the animals," he said.

"What animals?"

"The donkey, the sheep, the cow. Too bad they won't be able to make it to church on Sunday."

"That's blackmail."

"I never pretended to be perfect."

"You're not even *close*." Holly looked toward Loweva for support, but all she got was a smile so full of wicked glee that she wondered if Loweva hadn't been in on this little scheme all along. "Did you plan this with him?"

"It looks to me like he's man enough to do all his own devilment."

"All right. I'll go with you, Ben. But I don't plan to enjoy one single minute of your wretched company."

"I always did enjoy a woman with a stinger. Nice stinger, by the way," he said as she huffed past him.

At the door Holly turned. "Loweva, if I'm not back in an hour, call the police."

"Make that two," Ben said.

"One and a half."

"Deal."

TEN

Holly had never been inside a limousine. It had a bar, a television, even fresh roses in crystal vases. She stretched her legs out, reveling in the luxury of the soft leather seats.

Sitting opposite her, Ben smiled.

"I have a confession to make," she said.

"I'm listening."

"I lied a little. I'm already enjoying all this luxury."

"You might find other things to enjoy."

"Don't count on it." The driver started the car, and they glided forward so smoothly, they hardly seemed to be moving.

"Where's Hines?" Holly asked.

"Probably at home planning his lecture."

"What lecture?"

"The one he'll deliver to me when I get back."

Holly grinned. "He lectures you? About what?"

"Hines is old-fashioned. He won't approve of my behavior today."

"That makes two of us. Already I don't approve, and I don't even know what you're planning."

"On the contrary, Holly. I think you approve very much."

He gave her a sizzling look that would have curled her hair if it hadn't already been so curly. Her heart beat double time. Who was she trying to kid? She wasn't in this car so he would let his animals be in the live Nativity: she was in the limo because she wanted to be near Ben. He intrigued and excited her as no man ever had.

"Where are you taking me?"

"Where do you want to go?"

"Hmm, let me think about that. . . . New York, dinner at Tavern on the Green, then afterward a show."

Ben leaned forward. "Driver, the airport."

"Wait a minute, I didn't mean that."

"The next time, say what you mean." He changed the instructions with the driver. "I always give a lady what she wants, Holly. Remember that."

His threat made her feel deliciously naughty. Holly couldn't remember the last time she'd felt that way.

"All right, then, since we have this car and nearly an hour . . ."

"And a half," Ben added.

"Why don't we drive up the Natchez Trace? I've always loved that drive. It's quiet, it's beautiful, it's away from all the holiday hustle and bustle."

Ben instructed the driver, then leaned back in his seat.

"You're a woman of simple tastes, aren't you, Holly?"

"I've never given it much thought, but yes, I suppose I am."

"You like simple pleasure?"

"Yes."

"Like this."

Without warning, he caught her left ankle. She was wearing a long wool skirt and knee-length suede boots. He tugged off her boot and tossed it onto the seat beside him. Her ankle socks sported the Tasmanian Devil wearing a Santa hat and saying *Ho, ho, ho*.

"Cute socks," Ben said.

"What in the world are you doing?"

"Giving you a simple pleasure."

He stripped aside her sock and nestled her bare foot firmly against his crotch. Sexual currents of shocking power jolted through her.

"Stop that," she whispered.

"Don't you like it?"

"Yes . . . *No*. What if he sees?"

Ben's chuckle was deep and sexy. "Driver, pull into the next overlook we come to, then you can get out and take a break."

Ben ran the tip of his index finger from Holly's ankle to her toes.

"Is that better?" he said, releasing her foot.

"Yes . . . *No*. Oh . . . you're *wicked*."

"I try."

The car pulled off the Natchez Trace onto an overlook with a breathtaking view of majestic pines so green, you could almost smell them at a distance and, beyond that, brown fields lying fallow for the winter.

"Is this all right, Mr. Sullivan?" the driver asked.

"Perfect. Thank you."

Holly knew she should have protested when the driver got out of the car, but she didn't. She should have protested when Ben took off her other boot, but she didn't. She was too full of curiosity and excitement and half a dozen other emotions that she dared not think about, let alone name.

Alone in the car, Ben studied her in a way that stirred her blood. She could hear the rush of it thrumming in her ears.

What was the man up to?

The silence reverberated in the closed space, and still Ben didn't speak. If he meant to disturb her with his intense scrutiny, he had succeeded. If he meant to catch her off guard, he had failed. Holly prided herself on being equal to any occasion, and she was never without a quip handy.

She sought one now to relieve the tension.

"What's your plan? To keep me barefoot and pregnant?"

The minute the words were out of her mouth, she

knew she'd made a terrible mistake. But it was too late to take them back now, so she didn't even try.

"What an intriguing idea. Is that what you suggest?"

"Wipe that grin off your face. I'm suggesting no such thing. I'm merely trying to find some humor in this situation."

"That's important to you, isn't it, Holly, finding humor in situations that are difficult or scary?"

"Is that so bad?"

"No, not unless you use it as an excuse to hide your real feelings."

"If this is going to be a deep philosophical discussion, I'm going to put my boots back on. I can't think when my feet are cold."

"We can't let that happen. Come here."

Ben had her feet in his lap before she knew what was happening.

"There, is that better?"

How could she think with her bare feet snuggled tightly against his thighs? It took all her concentration just to *breathe*, particularly when he began a slow, erotic massage. As he stroked the palm of his hand against the sole of her feet, her toes curled under and she let out a soft little moan. She couldn't help herself.

"You like that, don't you?"

"If I lie, will you stop?"

"Depends."

"On what?"

"My mood."

He stroked her arch with his index finger, then began to trace small circles on her sensitive skin. It was extremely dangerous, that slow, erotic stroking. Ben instinctively knew what many men did not, that the foot was an erogenous zone.

Though reason had almost vanished, there was still a small voice inside Holly that questioned what she was doing in that car. She was a grown woman. She could demand that he stop that nonsense immediately and take her back where she belonged.

But why couldn't she belong in a limousine with a gorgeous man stroking her feet and making her feel attractive and desirable? What was wrong with letting go for just a few minutes and enjoying every deliciously wicked thing Ben Sullivan could do?

"Whatever you're doing, don't stop," she said.

Holly the vamp. Loweva would approve.

Ben's laughter was low and sexy. "I think it's called groveling. Is this what you had in mind?"

"Not exactly . . . but it will do."

Ben uncapped the small bottle of lotion, and the scent of roses surrounded them. Such a romantic fragrance. Exactly right with the heat in the car, so much heat that Holly couldn't tell what was on the outside of her body and what was on the inside. Delicious heat. After years of doing without, she reveled in the sensation.

She watched while he heated the lotion in his palms. Erotic images came to mind, images of Ben rubbing the lotion not only on her feet but on her calves, behind her knees, inside her thighs. Slick flesh caressing slick flesh. Hot skin touching hot skin.

Slowly she drew her tongue over her full bottom lip.

"That's incredibly sexy," Ben said.

"I didn't mean it to be."

"Didn't you?"

The truth was, she did. Perhaps not consciously, but certainly unconsciously. She knew she was deprived, but she had never thought of herself as depraved.

Holly the seductress. She didn't need anybody's approval. *She* liked it. She liked it very much.

"Actually, I did," she confessed. "I figured that as long as I'm your captive, I might as well make the best of it."

He laughed. "At last, an honest woman. I thought they were a dying breed."

"Not where I come from."

"Your honesty deserves a reward."

He cupped her left foot between his hands and began a heady massage. Suddenly she was drowning in sensation, heat from his thigh, heat from his hands, heat coming from deep inside her.

She had always believed that the only chemistry was the kind you had to struggle through your freshman year at college. Her two husbands had done nothing to change her mind.

Now she knew better. Chemistry was a steamroller: It ran over you when you least expected. It was something that came out of nowhere and simply overpowered you. Not merely overpowered you, but filled you and charged you and changed you, inside and out.

Holly surrendered to the chemistry. Leaning back in her seat, she wiggled her toes and made soft humming sounds of sheer ecstasy.

"I like a woman who is not afraid to express her pleasure."

"I like a man who gives it."

"How can I reward you for that?" His hands slid over her ankles and halfway up her calf. She wondered if it was possible to die of too much pleasure.

"Will this do?" he said.

His voice was soft and intimate. He probably talked that way to every woman he met, but she wasn't going to think about that right now.

"Oh, yes," she said. "That will do very nicely."

Holly the hot hoyden. If her conscience pricked her the tiniest bit for betraying her friends the Snipeses, she would deal with that tomorrow.

Holly O'Hara. The only difference between her and Scarlett being that she didn't have an eighteen-inch waist—and never would, even with a waist cincher.

What Ben was doing with her legs was probably a sin of some kind and definitely should be outlawed. He was stroking them in a way that sent shivers over her.

Were his hands sliding higher? Yes, definitely. Almost to the knee.

Would he go beyond? More to the point, would she let him?

Oh, Lordy, she shouldn't, but she probably would, considering her present absence of mind. That combined with overpowering chemistry was lethal.

How high under her skirts could she let him reach before she crossed the line between proper and improper? And did it count if nobody saw?

The absurdity of her line of thinking suddenly struck her, and she chuckled.

"Ticklish?" he said.

"No . . . oh, no." Once something turned her tickle box over, Holly had a hard time stopping her laughter.

"I didn't know I was doing a comedy routine."

His wounded male pride was showing. That added to her hilarity.

"It's . . . not . . . you," she gasped between giggles.

"Then what is it?"

"Me."

With the lift of one eyebrow, he demanded an explanation.

"I was sitting here trying to decide if the likes of Miss Manners had ever declared a line of demarcation." His eyebrow lifted a notch higher. "You know, to separate the proper ladies from the improper ones. And then I was wondering which side I would fall on, and whether I even cared . . . and I got tickled."

There was nothing as sobering as being closely observed by a sexy man. Holly's laughter ceased as abruptly as it had begun. To make matters worse, she couldn't even remember why she had found all that so funny in the first place.

"Fascinating," he said, without a single hint of sarcasm.

"What?" she whispered, for suddenly she realized that his hands were still on her leg, and that if he kept up those slow sensual movements for another thirty seconds, she was going to stretch out on the leather seats of that white stretch limousine and start writhing and moaning in a very improper fashion.

"You," he said. "My original observation still stands: When you find a situation difficult or frightening, you use humor to keep from facing your real feelings. Do I scare you, Holly?"

The scariest thing about him was his razor-sharp mind. He could see through every smoke screen she dreamed up.

She jerked out of his grasp and grabbed her boots. "No, you don't scare me, not in the least."

She rammed her feet into her boots, careful to keep her freshly massaged and still tingling legs covered by her long wool skirt.

"Your time is up," she said.

She half expected him to protest. Instead he politely requested that the driver return to the car and take them back to the church. Then he settled back into his seat with an enigmatic smile on his face.

There was no use trying to figure him out. Even after all their encounters, he remained a man of mystery. He puzzled her, maddened her, and absolutely fascinated her.

When he caught her studying him, he winked.

"There's something to be said for groveling," he said in that deep, rich voice that made her hot and cold all at the same time. "Don't you agree?"

"Yes, but I wouldn't say it in polite company."

He chuckled. "By all means, say it. The company is not polite."

"Speak for yourself. Our driver is extremely polite, and I'm a lady from the top of my head to the tip of my toes."

"I can vouch for the head and the toes. The interesting part is going to be finding out about everything in between."

Ben was playing games, and she decided to play along. Batting her eyelashes Scarlett O'Hara fashion, she practically purred, "Why, Mr. Sullivan. How you turn a girl's head with your pretty lies."

"That's not a lie; it's a promise."

Holly had spent a number of lonely years trying to erase the empty promises her two ex-husbands had made. The thing that took her so aback about Ben was that his promise didn't seem empty. Oh, he was playing with her, there was no doubt about that. Having a bit of fun in this fancy limousine with the fresh roses in real crystal vases.

But somehow the things he said had the ring of truth. Not that she was any expert, but she had learned that sometimes you could look in a man's eyes and see whether he was making up pretty lies to suit the occasion or saying things he meant.

Ben meant every word he said. For once, Holly was all out of quips.

ELEVEN

Somewhere in the distance Christmas bells were ringing, but Ben was definitely not in a Christmas mood. He was down at his barn trying to coax Henry into the trailer he had rented for the occasion. The donkey, being his usual obnoxious self, refused to budge. To top it all off, it had rained the night before, and Ben was standing ankle-deep in mud.

Besides all that, he was still in a foul mood from Hines's lecture. True to his nature, Hines had upbraided Ben royally about taking Holly out in the limousine without calling her first. *Kidnapping* was his word for it.

"That's no way to treat a lady, sir."

There was no telling what Hines would have said if he had known about the foot massage. What he didn't know wouldn't hurt him.

Ben wasn't courting the woman; he was merely

researching her, testing her. So far, she was making top-notch scores.

The thought of seeing her again made him feel good in a clean, wholesome way. He could hardly wait.

"Look, Henry. We don't have all day. If it's good enough for the sheep, it ought to be good enough for you."

He tugged on Henry's halter, but the donkey stood his ground, expressing his opinion with a loud bray.

"I don't think you can sway a donkey with reason, sir."

Dressed in suit and tie, Hines stood under a huge umbrella well out of reach of the mud and mayhem in the barn.

"I'm don't need advice from a man whose shoes still bear a spit shine."

Ben's own boots were beyond redemption. He even had mud on his jeans.

"Be that as it may, sir, *somebody* has to come up with a plan or else we'll be late delivering these beasts to the church."

"We're not going to be late, even if I have to bodily lift that stubborn animal into the truck."

"We might call on some of the neighbors for help. That farmer down the road seems a nice sort."

When Ben had told Holly that he was part of the deal, he'd never dreamed that transporting the animals would be such a problem. But he had never seen a problem that he couldn't solve, and he wasn't about to start now.

"I said I would do this, and I'm going to do it. I'm not about to let a jackass get the best of me."

"My sentiments exactly. Don't let the beast get the best of you, sir."

Ben tired of friendly persuasion and tried force. But the donkey dug his hooves into the mud and wouldn't be moved. A cow watching with interest from the other side of the pasture fence let her sentiments be known with a soulful mooing.

"I don't need advice from you, either," Ben said, and then he remembered what Holly had told about the cow and the donkey being inseparable.

"Hines, if you'll open that pasture gate and let Gertrude out, I think this problem will be solved."

Ben put a small pile of hay just inside the trailer, and Gertrude marched docilely in. Henry promptly joined his best friend, and Ben latched the tailer gate.

"Very impressive, sir."

"If you can get this rig up to the house while I make a quick change, we'll be off. Can you drive this thing?"

"Nothing to it, sir. I've watched a lot of cowboy movies."

The tables in the Fellowship Hall were laid with juice and doughnuts, the Christmas decorations were in place, and the live Nativity was ready for the animals.

"Where's Ben?" Loweva said.

Over the intercom they could hear the minister still going full blast with his sermon. Early church wouldn't be over for another thirty minutes. They still had plenty of time to get the animals in place.

"Don't worry," Holly said. "He promised he would come, and he always keeps his promises."

If Loweva thought it odd that Holly was defending a man she had once considered the enemy, she wisely kept her thoughts to herself.

"And where's Grace?" Loweva grumbled. "If you ask me, she's the one ought to be here seeing about this foolish piece of business since she's the one who thought it all up. How come you always get stuck with these dirty jobs?"

"I like to think of it as being chosen because of my brilliant and uncanny knack for being in charge."

Sometimes Holly wished she didn't get tapped to do so many odd jobs for every department in the church, but she never said no. In a way it was flattering that Jonathan thought she was equal to almost any task.

Suddenly the door opened and Ben Sullivan strode through.

"Are you the angel in charge?" He stood directly in front of her, raking her from head to toe with his black eyes.

Holly had to remind herself that she was in church and should act accordingly.

"Yes. I always enter the spirit of the season," she

said, explaining her costume. "Besides, the kids love my costumes."

"So do I."

His gaze was slow, deliberate, and sexy. At that moment Holly wanted to be anywhere except church.

"You brought the animals?" she said.

"*All* of them."

His eyes raked her once more, and she marveled at how a man could turn a woman inside out with nothing more than a single look. That single look caught and held her, and as they stood in the middle of the Fellowship Hall wrapped in hot silence, Holly knew that once in a lifetime there comes a man who can render a woman speechless. Ben Sullivan was that man. After today she could no longer tell herself that he was the enemy. She could no longer pretend that she was merely intrigued by him or that she was simply playing games.

The only game she wanted to play with Ben Sullivan was for keeps. While she had deluded herself that she could slip and slide toward a fatal attraction but never take a tumble, she had fallen. Hard.

It no longer mattered what he had done or who he was. It no longer mattered that he was probably wrong for her or that she was probably making another terrible mistake. Her heart was out of control. All she could do was pray that she didn't get hurt, and that if she did, she could pick up the pieces and put them back together again without too many of the damaged parts showing.

Meanwhile early church was in full swing, the coffee was perking, and the season to make merry was at hand. Thank goodness Holly had plenty to take her mind off the delicious man standing in front of her—at least for a little while.

"Bring the animals in here," she said.

"In the Fellowship Hall?"

"Grace, the director of the children's department, fixed a place for them yesterday. Over there." Holly pointed.

Sixteen kindergarten-size chairs had been arranged in a large semicircle in front of the west wall. Looped along the tops of the chairs was a length of rope.

"I'm just a city slicker, but I don't think those little chairs are going to prove much of a barrier for two sheep, a cow, and a donkey."

"We'll wrangle them," Holly said with more confidence than she felt. "Better get them in here. The early-church crowd will soon be here for doughnuts and coffee."

"Whatever you say, boss angel," he said, then headed toward the door.

Holly discovered a simple truth: People in love have an uncanny knack for finding significance in every word of their beloved. She glowed at the way Ben called her *boss angel*, as if the boss part was a compliment to her talent for organization, and the angel part was an endearment meant especially for her.

From across the room she watched as Ben came in with his animals, and while she watched she wondered if Loweva noticed anything different about her.

Was it possible for a best friend to know when someone had stolen her heart?

The two sheep were docile enough. Hines followed along as Ben led them inside their makeshift stall. Then he pulled up a chair beside the coffeepot and sat down.

"You're not coming to help me bring in Henry and Gertrude?" Ben asked.

"It's your show, sir. All I want is a ringside seat."

"Desertion in my hour of need. I'll remember that, Hines."

"I'm not worried, sir. I'm the one who writes the checks."

Holly watched the interchange between Ben and his employee with great interest. It was a side of the man she had never seen, a warm, easy side that was extraordinarily appealing.

Ben left to get the other animals, while Holly and Loweva filled large stainless-steel trays with doughnuts. Grace and her husband, Marvin, breezed through the door, Grace dressed to the nines in black crepe and pearls and Marvin looking his best in a pinstripe suit and tie.

Grace went immediately to the sheep.

"How cute! Won't the children love them?" She turned to Holly. "Where are the rest of the animals?"

"Coming through the door even as we speak."

Ben held two halters, leading the Christmas donkey and his cohort, Gertrude the cow. The donkey stepped gingerly along, looking pleased to be the center of so much attention.

But Gertrude had a different attitude. The Fellowship Hall was not at all like the barn she was used to, and furthermore, it didn't have a dirt floor. The minute her sharp hooves met the slick tiles, her legs went in all four directions. Six hundred pounds of cow hit the floor with a plop.

Over the intercom the congregation was singing "Joy to the World." But it wasn't joy reigning in the Fellowship Hall: It was consternation.

"What are we going to do?" Grace said, turning to Holly.

"Get the donkey into the roped-off area, and then we'll deal with the cow." Holly had no idea how to deal with a cow sprawled on the floor, but she was bound to think of something.

It was easier said than done. With Gertrude in the middle of the floor, Henry refused to budge. Ben tugged and coaxed to no avail. Marvin came along to help, but the two of them were no match in a tug-of-war with a stubborn donkey.

"If we had a carrot, we might coax him," Ben said.

"We don't have any carrots," Holly said. "What about a doughnut?"

"Do donkeys eat doughnuts?" Grace asked.

"We won't know until we try." Holly got two doughnuts and offered them to Henry. "Here you go, sweetheart," she said, patting his head. Henry rolled his eyes. "Come on, try it. You might like it."

Henry took a nibble, rolled his eyes some more, then suddenly stretched his neck out for another bite.

With Ben holding the halter and Holly leading the way, they got Henry to join the sheep.

"Well done, Holly," Ben said.

She couldn't have been more pleased if he had given her a dozen red roses.

"I'm a woman of many talents," she said, then blushed at her own audacity.

"We'll have to see about that," he murmured, for her ears only.

She might have been caught up in his spell once more if it hadn't been for the intercom. The congregation was belting out the last verse of "Joy to the World," and she and her coworkers didn't have a minute to lose.

The cow was still on the floor, and she didn't have any idea what to do about it. To buy time, she gave Henry the last doughnut.

While the final verse of "Joy to the World" played over the intercom, Henry stretched out for the doughnut.

"Lordy have mercy." Loweva said. "I've been here for fifteen years, and I've never seen no donkey eating doughnuts in this church."

"No, but I've seen a lot of jackasses eating doughnuts in here," Marvin said.

Grace tugged his sleeve. "Behave yourself, Marvin. Put your legal mind to work getting that cow off the floor." Without waiting for him to come up with a solution, she turned to Holly. "What are we going to *do*?" she wailed.

"We'll never get the damned cow off the floor," Marvin said, paying Grace back for her lack of faith in him. "There's not enough traction."

"I have an idea." Holly raced to the door, opened it, and dragged in a rubber floor mat. "Let's gather all these and make some traction."

Ben and Hines watched while Grace and Marvin and Loweva and Holly scattered in four different directions.

"This is quite a show, sir," Hines said.

"A regular three-ring circus," Ben said. "Do you think it's like this every Sunday? Almost makes me want to come to find out."

"Miss Jones is rather fetching in that angel garb, did you notice?"

"I noticed."

"I thought you might." Hines grinned, then helped himself to a cup of coffee. "She has a great personality too. Makes you feel warm just being in her presence."

"Don't overdo it, Hines. Sometimes subtlety is the best approach."

"I'll try to remember that, sir."

Holly and her crew returned with the floor mats. With her directing, the others spread the mats around the cow. Grace and Marvin kept up a running verbal battle, with Grace cajoling the cow and Marvin pointing out the errors of her ways.

"Conversation with a bovine is useless, Grace," he said.

"How do you know that, Marvin? Have you ever tried it?"

"No, and I don't plan to start now."

"Well, *somebody's* got to get the cow off the floor."

Loweva rolled her eyes. "I've known of cows who sulled up when they was down like this, just sulled up and refused to move for days. Sometimes it took a tractor to get them up."

"Think positive, Loweva," Holly said. "She's going to get up so she can be a part of the live Nativity, aren't you, Gertrude?"

But Gertrude had other ideas. All the excitement finally proved too much for her, and she relieved some of her tension—right in the middle of the floor.

"Oh, dear," Grace said. "What do we do now?"

"I know what I'm gonna do." Loweva escaped to the kitchen.

"Mops, buckets," Holly said, not yet daunted, but close. In the kitchen she cornered her assistant. "Loweva, there will be a little something extra in your Christmas stocking if you'll help us clean this mess up."

"Holly, is there anything you've asked me to do in all these years we've been working together that I refused?"

"Nothing."

Loweva picked up the dishcloth and started wiping counters that were already clean.

"Well, today is the first. I'm not cleaning up after no cow."

"What are we going to do now, Holly?" Grace said.

Scream, Holly wanted to say.

At this moment Marvin developed a sudden interest in the coffeepot, and Grace was standing around in her high heels and pearls looking helpless. Holly wished she had that option. She was intrepid and resourceful and happily independent . . . most of the time. Occasionally, though, it would be nice to throw up her hands and say, *I can't*, or lean on a broad shoulder and have someone pat her head and say *Honey, don't worry about a thing; I'll take care of that*, or even to sit in a quiet corner and cry.

As much as she might like to attribute her mood to the season, with all its expectations, she was honest enough to know that Ben Sullivan was the cause. Even with the Fellowship Hall in total uproar, he was more on her mind than the problem at hand.

Was it possible for him to know what was happening to her heart just by looking? And would he run if he knew?

Holly didn't want him to run. Even if he never knew how she felt, even if he never felt the same, she didn't want to lose Ben. Even when they had been enemies, being with him was fun and exhilarating.

Her life hadn't been drab before he came. She had too many friends and too many interests for her life to be called colorless. But there was a vast difference between having fun with female friends and having fun with a man. No experience was quite as heady as a lively give-and-take between a man and a woman.

Almost no experience, Holly corrected herself. But she wasn't even going to think about that one, especially not today.

Yes, she definitely wanted to scream, but not because of the cow.

As if he had read her thoughts, Ben approached her and put a hand on her elbow. It was just a small touch, nothing significant when she thought of all the ways a man could touch a woman, and yet it steadied her, calmed her.

"I'll help," he said.

"You don't have to do this, you know," Holly said.

"Even Scrooge was nice at Christmas."

"I think you've outdone Scrooge."

"Does that mean my approval rating has gone up?"

"The jury's still out."

"I've never known a woman like you."

"Is that good or bad?"

He grinned. "The jury's still out."

They finished the task as early church was drawing to a close. Over the intercom the minister spoke the benediction. In a few minutes hundreds of people would pour into the Fellowship Hall for coffee and doughnuts.

"Listen. . . ." Grace cocked her head. "Oh, Lord, I wish I'd never had this idea. How will we ever explain a cow in the middle of the floor?"

Her distress brought out Holly's earth-mother side. She patted Grace's arm.

"Remember, the opera's not over till the fat lady sings."

Over the intercom the choir sang the first notes of the benediction.

"Looks like that fat lady you talking about is fixing to cut loose," Loweva drawled.

"I have an idea," Holly said. "We'll cover the cow's legs with hay, and she'll look like she's praying."

Ben cocked an eyebrow. "You should be in D.C. You'd fit right in." Then, smiling, he headed toward the coffeepot.

"Great idea," Grace said. "Come on, Marvin. . . ."

They grabbed armfuls of hay from the roped off area and tossed them at the cow. Back and forth they scurried, while the last note of the benediction echoed through the hall.

"Amen," the minister pronounced in his mellifluous voice.

Slowly Gertrude rose, then with a toss of her head she joined Henry in the makeshift stall. Her exhausted audience clapped and cheered.

"Divine intervention," Loweva quipped.

"Loweva!" Holly said.

"When I'm bad, I'm very bad." Loweva winked, then nodded toward Ben Sullivan, who was staring at Holly over the rim of his coffee cup. "Like that one over yonder. Seems like somebody who would come calling in a white limousine is worthy of a little trouble. Maybe you ought to give him a try."

"I don't have time," Holly quipped. "I'm too busy taking care of things."

She wasn't deliberately being deceitful. Humor was an automatic response to cover feelings that were too private to share.

TWELVE

The file folder was marked *Holly Jones.* It wasn't as thick as the others in Ben's filing cabinet, but he didn't need her vote on a crucial issue.

Or maybe he did. Was kissing crucial? Cuddling? Making slow sweet love in his brass bed while the sun slanted through the window?

He glanced over the information he had on her. She'd been orphaned at six months, raised by her paternal grandmother, earned a teaching degree, then taught kindergarten for two years before becoming a church social director. All in Mississippi.

On the other hand, her brother James had gone to school at Harvard, then worked in Boston, New York, and Chicago before settling in Memphis, Tennessee, with his wife and two children. He was a senior partner in the law firm of Michaels, Curtis, and Jones, and he had six Appaloosas on his large estate in Germantown, three of the horses award-winners.

Holly was obviously a very intelligent woman. Besides that, she had a creative mind. Ben chuckled thinking of all the solutions she'd come up with for getting the cow off the floor.

Then why hadn't Holly had all the advantages of her brother James? Had she had a choice?

More to the point, why had Ben spent the last half hour mulling over Holly's family problems. He couldn't solve his own, let alone hers.

Disgusted with himself, he tossed the manila folder onto his desk. It landed beside an expensive linen-finished envelope with a Boston postmark. A letter from home. No, not a letter. An engraved invitation.

Ben picked up the envelope and pulled out the invitation. *You are invited for Christmas dinner at the home of Mr. and Mrs. Benjamin G. Sullivan II on December 24th at seven P.M. at Number Six, Beacon Hill.* There was no personal note, no signature scrawled in ink, nothing. Just a printed card sent to their only son, probably with the fervent hope that he wouldn't come to spoil their day.

Every June he made the obligatory annual visit home; he didn't owe them his holidays, bleak as they were. But bleak was better than the alternative. Bleak was better than the armed truce that always degenerated into a pitched battle. His parents should have divorced years ago and spared each other so much misery, but they clung to the pitiful remains of their marriage because of money and social prestige. Together they were dazzling jet-setters, flamboyant hosts of fabulous parties, a power couple sought out by photographers wherever they went. Apart they would be just another divorced set of moguls squabbling over the division of a media empire.

No, Ben would not be accepting the holiday invitation of Mr. and Mrs. Benjamin G. Sullivan II, not this year, not any year.

The contrast between them and Holly Jones was tremendous. They were jaded and brittle, she was vivacious and warm; they could dissemble in six languages, she spoke the simple truth in one. Or did she? Was she the sweet innocent she seemed to be or another barracuda hiding in an angel costume?

The front door opened and a gust of wind blew in, bringing a refreshing coolness and Hines, bundled up from head to toe.

"You look like the Abominable Snowman."

"It's nippy out today, sir."

"That's a Mississippi winter for you, sixty degrees one day and twenty the next. What were you doing out in it, anyhow?"

"Looking for a Christmas tree."

"Why? I never have a tree."

"It's high time you did. Besides, hanging decorations then taking them off again will give you something to do while I'm in Virginia for Christmas."

"Where's the tree?"

"Out in the back forty. It's perfect, sir, about five feet tall, symmetrical branches, no bare spots. It's waiting for you to dig it up and wrap the roots in burlap. You can replant it after Christmas."

"That's a lot of trouble for a tree."

"Some things are worth the trouble. Miss Jones, for instance." Hines walked to the desk. "I see you're studying her file."

"Don't make an issue of it. I always study files before I enter into negotiations."

"What sort of negotiations?"

"I was thinking of asking her to be my date for Senator Glenn's fund-raising dinner."

"Don't you think all that research takes a little of the romance out of it, sir?"

"I don't believe in romance, Hines. I believe in being prepared."

"If I recall, all the great lovers of history followed their hearts instead of their heads."

"They paid for their mistakes. Most of them died the hard way."

"Be that as it may, I think planning takes all the fun out of dating."

"Going out to dinner can hardly be classified as dating. Besides, this is not personal. I merely need a date."

Hines smiled. "Shall I get the shovel, sir?"

"The shovel?"

"For the tree."

Why had she ever said yes?

The purple velvet that had been perfect for Loweva's nephew's winter wedding was all wrong for an important political fund-raiser. Did she have time to change?

Holly glanced at her watch. Ten minutes. Not enough time. Besides, there was nothing else in her closet that was even remotely appropriate except the red satin she'd made five years ago for the Sunday-school Christmas party. It would be even worse than the purple velvet.

She went into the den where Lily was ensconced in her favorite chair with the television going full blast. It was an insipid game show. Holly turned down the volume, then did a pirouette in front of her grandmother.

"What do you think, Lily?"

"It makes your hips look big."

Holly was an expert at covering pain with laughter, and she proved it once more.

"Everything makes my hips look big," she quipped, "even the bathtub."

"Where are you going anyway?"

"I already told you, Grandma. Birmingham. There's a party in Birmingham."

"I don't see how come you have to go all the way to Alabama to a party when Jean Grimes is having one right down the street."

"It's not a Christmas party; it's a political fund-raiser."

"Just as long as you're back in time to turn on my electric blanket. You know I don't like a cold bed. It makes my feet cold, and when my feet are cold I have nightmares."

"Loweva's coming over later to bring your dinner and turn on your blanket. She'll be here all night, Grandma."

"Where's she going to sleep?"

"In my bedroom."

Lily pursed her lips and shook her head. "It's not right. James wouldn't leave me with strangers."

This time Holly couldn't force a laugh, not even a small one.

"Well, James is not here, Lily. Loweva will have to do."

"I hope I don't get sick while you're gone."

"If you do, Loweva will take care of you."

"What if I have to go to the doctor?"

"She has a car." And then, because Holly felt guilty for being so curt, she sat beside her grand-mother and took her hand. "It's a white Cadillac, Grandma. You'll love it."

"I don't like Cadillacs," Lily said, and Holly knew it was useless. No matter what she said, Lily was go-ing to find fault. There was no way that Holly could leave for even one day with a clear conscience, let alone Lily's blessing.

She glanced at her watch. There were still five minutes left . . . if Ben arrived on time—and he didn't look like the kind of man with a cavalier atti-tude about time. Five minutes to think about wearing the wrong kind of dress that made her hips look big. Five minutes to wish she'd said no. Five minutes to wish she'd had two weeks before the party to diet instead of two days.

Speaking of which, she was starving. To top it all off she felt as if her stomach was going to growl. Wouldn't that be mortifying?

"Hello, Senator Whosis, my name is Holly and that other greeting you hear is my stomach."

She was so nervous, she had forgotten the senator's name. Graden? Gibson? Grover? Something with a *G*.

Maybe she should eat a cracker before Ben came. Her hand was in the cracker box when the doorbell rang. That's all she needed—Ben Sullivan to find her eating.

She closed her eyes for a second and imagined herself slim, sophisticated, and scintillating. If she could get through the rest of the day, she swore to God and herself and her mother and everybody else who counted that she would start a serious diet tomorrow.

But tomorrow night was Loweva's Christmas party, and her pecan tassies were the best in the state. Then there was the Sunday-school ice-cream party, and after that the senior citizens' Christmas Dessert Extravaganza.

She would start Tuesday. Definitely Tuesday.

The doorbell pinged again. Leaving Ben Sullivan standing out in the cold was not the way to start a date.

Long ago Holly had learned that if she put on a fancy smile, people didn't notice that she was scared and uncertain. "Look at that smile," they'd say. "Holly Jones has the world by the tail."

With her most brilliant smile in place, she swung the door open, but the minute she saw Ben Sullivan every ounce of bravado she'd managed to work up suddenly deserted her. In suit and tie he was gorgeous; in a tuxedo he was lethal.

Her wits left her, and she said the first thing that came to her mind.

"You are dangerous and must be destroyed."

"I can think of a number of exciting ways for you to do that," he said.

Holly felt her cheeks go hot. "That's an old habit, saying the first thing that pops into my mind. Don't worry, though. I promise not to embarrass you with that kind of remark."

"On the contrary. Hearing people say what they really think is a novelty. If you'll do that at the political function, it will not only be a refreshing change, it might relieve the tedium."

Visions of riding across the state line with soft music playing and Ben reaching for her hand suddenly vanished. He had made his intentions clear during the phone call: He needed a date. Still she had persisted in thinking of this outing as a romantic evening. Foolish dreams of a foolish woman.

"That's a tall order," she quipped, "relieving the tedium of three hundred people, but I'm equal to the task." She held the door wide. "Won't you come in and meet my grandmother." When he hesitated, she winked. "Don't be scared. She bites, but it's not life threatening."

Her house was neither fancy nor fine, but it was

sparkling clean and it had a homey charm all its own.
Holly was fond of candid snapshots, and there were
always cheap frames to be had at flea markets and
garage sales. She liked being able to look almost anywhere in her house and be greeted by the smiling face
of one of her friends.

She loved flowers, too, and had a knack not only
for growing them but for preserving the dried blos-
soms. Roses that still held a hint of the vivid pink they
possessed when Holly had them delivered to Lily for
her birthday last year topped the drop-leaf table on
the west wall. Baby's breath, which dried so well, was
intertwined with dried purple violets in a small grape-
vine wreath that hung over the TV.

If Ben found fault with her house, she was going
to march into her bedroom and remove her tacky
purple velvet dress and tell him to go relieve the tedium by himself. Only when he nodded his approval
did she realize how tense she was.

He was equally gracious when she introduced him
to Lily. Unfortunately, she couldn't say the same for
her grandmother.

"I don't approve of Yankees," she said.

"I live here now," Ben said. "Maybe Mississippi
will smooth out my rough edges."

"You have a glib tongue, young man. See that you
don't use it on Holly. She's prone to fool notions."

"That's excellent advice, and I'm sure your grand-
daughter will see that I don't misbehave, ma'am."

Lily warmed a little. Who wouldn't? Ben's smile

would thaw icebergs, and his use of politeness and formality was a clever ploy.

On more than one occasion Ben had told Holly that he was dangerous. With Lily he proved it once more. When he bent over her hand, he outdid Rhett Butler for true Southern charm.

"Ready to go, Holly?" he said.

"Yes," she said, knowing it was a lie.

How could she ever be ready for such a dangerous man?

THIRTEEN

Three hours in a car with a woman was a long time, long enough to discover things not only about Holly but about himself as well. For instance, Ben had prided himself on the careful research job he was doing regarding Holly. He had told himself that this trip to the political rally would be one more chance to unmask her as a consummate actress if not a downright opportunist. After all, a woman in her position could do worse than land a man of his considerable wealth and influence.

What he hadn't counted on was the effect her perfume would have on him in close quarters. One whiff of her fragrance and research went right out of his mind. Instead he thought how pleasant it would be to sit beside a roaring fire with her and bury his face in the soft white curve between her neck and her shoulder. Without asking, he knew she had spritzed perfume there.

"What is that fragrance?" he asked.

"Do you like it?"

Her artless question took him by surprise. It was a totally feminine response, one he found utterly delightful.

"Yes, I like it. It reminds me of flowers."

"That's what it's supposed to do. It's ginger lily. My brother got it for me in Hawaii."

Had she worn that perfume just for him? The thought pleased Ben.

"Have you been to Hawaii, Holly?"

"Not yet. But someday I will. I want to see the whales."

"I expected you to say you wanted to see the flowers or the beaches or even the volcanoes. Why the whales?"

"I don't know. Maybe it's because they travel all that distance so they can breed in the warm waters of a tropical paradise. There's something beautiful and terribly romantic about that."

Ben took note: Holly loved romance. She was the kind of woman who would enjoy flowers on Valentine's Day and perfume on her birthday. Not that any of that mattered, of course. He wasn't about to do anything so foolish as send flowers and perfume to a woman who took romance seriously.

He glanced her way and caught her studying him. There was a glow in her eyes that he found disturbing. Quickly he returned his attention to the road, and she reached over to turn up the volume on the radio. A nice easy blues tune was playing. Holly hummed along softly, and he tried to concentrate on the road.

But the sweet way she smelled kept intruding. And the way she hummed, low and throaty and sexy. And the way her hair looked in the late-afternoon sun pouring through her side of the window.

"Not that I believe in all those romantic myths," she said. "For whales or people, either."

"Of course not. Neither do I."

"I mean . . . anybody who has been divorced twice should know better. Right?"

"Absolutely. I agree with you."

She turned up the radio another notch, then settled into silence on her side of the car. Though she wasn't pouting, and even glanced his way every now and then to smile, Ben felt a sense of loss, as if he had let something precious slip by.

"Sooo," she said, finally breaking the silence, her voice soft and breathless as if she were running all the way from Tupelo to Birmingham instead of traveling along in the comfort of a car. "I've never been to an important political rally. Tell me what to expect."

Talking about politics was safe and familiar, but Ben missed their talk of perfume and ginger lilies and whales and paradise. He told her about some of the rallies he had attended in the past, and even made some of the stories funny. Funnier than they warranted. With a few exceptions, he had hated that aspect of his job. He found the ostentatious display of money repugnant and the pseudo-intellectualism boring.

Because of their long drive, the rally was in full swing when they arrived. Crowds thronged around the buffet tables and a dance band was playing music with a good beat.

"A band," Holly said. "How wonderful!"

How many women would be happy over such a small thing? None that he knew.

"Would you like to dance?" he said, surprising himself. He didn't even like to dance. Couldn't, as a matter of fact. "I have to warn you, I'm not any good at this. I'm liable to step all over your feet."

"I'll take my chances."

The way she fit into his arms was too good to be true. Suddenly he realized that every game he had played with her had been a prelude to this moment, a carefully orchestrated plan to get close enough to feel the seductive curve of her breasts and the soft slide of her hips as they danced on the polished floor.

She wore her hair loose, and it was as silky as he had imagined. The subtle fragrance of ginger lily wafted from those soft strands. If he weren't careful, he would be burying his nose in her hair.

He didn't know the name of the song the band played, but it was something that didn't require a lot of moving around.

"Why, you're a good dancer," she said.

"Who wouldn't be with you? You have a natural rhythm."

"Thank you."

Would that rhythm translate from the dance floor to the bedroom? He loosened his hold and put some distance between their hips so she wouldn't know the effect she had on him.

This business of dancing was dangerous. Men bent on avoiding such things as romance and love and marriage should avoid it at all costs.

He hoped the song would soon end. No sooner had the last note died than he released her.

"That about does it for me," he said. "I guess I'm a one-dance man."

"I'm glad that dance was with me."

Every time Holly made one of those sweet, artless remarks Ben wanted to kiss her. If she kept it up, he was going to be in deep trouble.

Fortunately, Senator Marion Glenn and his wife, Ginger, arrived and saved him. Ben made the introductions, and small talk followed. He hated small talk. When the Senator's wife drew him aside to inquire whether he thought his alma mater would be a suitable school for her youngest son, he was more than happy to shift conversational gears.

During his years in D.C., Ben had mastered the art of listening to two conversations at once and never missing a word. While he conversed with the senator's wife, he heard everything that was said by Holly and the senator.

She was relating the story of the cow in the Fellowship Hall, with frequent pauses for the senator's bursts of laughter.

"And then the preacher said the benediction, and Gertrude arose like a martyred saint." More laughter from the senator. "Loweva said it was divine intervention."

"My dear, I haven't laughed so much in years. Where in the world has our Benjamin been keeping you?"

"Oh, I keep myself, as well as my grandmother Lily and a parrot who never says a word except *help*."

"I'm sure you have a delightful explanation as to why that bird has such a limited vocabulary."

As she launched into another funny story Holly's face glowed with happiness and good humor. What a contrast she was to all the other women Ben had dated. What a contrast to his mother.

Her story of the parrot ended, and the senator put his arm around her shoulders.

"My dear, you're a gold mine. If Ben's smart, he'll stake out his claim before some other fellow snatches you up." Taking Holly's arm, Marion Glenn joined his wife and Ben. "Did you hear that, Ben? I know you did. You never miss a trick."

"I heard."

Holly's cheeks were bright pink, and there was a barely perceptible line of moisture on her upper lip. For some reason that telltale glow lifted Ben's spirits. Women in D.C. society didn't allow themselves to sweat.

The senator clapped him on the arm. "You're the same old Ben, I see. Nobody on Capitol Hill ever had an inkling of what you thought or where you stood until you quietly slipped in and slit their throats, then left them bleeding on the floor. That's what made you so damned good at your job."

"I'm afraid life in the slow lane has destroyed my killer instincts."

"Once a shark, always a shark." Senator Glenn swiveled to smile at Holly. "And I mean that in the most complimentary of ways, my dear."

"Pay him no mind," Ben said to Holly. "Men on the campaign trail will say anything to get what they want."

"I guess you know what it is that I want, don't you, Ben?"

"Yes, Senator. And you already know the answer to that."

"I need you, my boy."

"There are other lobbyists who can get the job done."

"But not with your subtlety, not with your class."

"I'm just a farmer."

"You'll never be just a farmer. You'll never be *just* anything. You're the best, and if I'm going to get reelected, I need the best handling of that farm subsidy bill on the floor." The senator caught Ben's arm. "Don't say no yet, not till you've heard my story." Turning to Holly and his wife, he said, "My dears, do you mind if Ben and I slip off for a quiet talk?"

Ginger Glenn smiled at her husband. "Darling, if I panicked every time you *slipped away*, I'd have divorced you long ago." She pecked him affectionately on the cheek. "Be convincing, Senator."

Ben missed nothing of their exchange, all the

while keeping his eyes on Holly. In a crowd of women sporting designer gowns and a king's ransom in jewels, she made a statement of simplicity and elegance. In the midst of the brittle laughter and the false smiles, her spontaneity and charm were as refreshing as cool rain on a scorching summer day.

She turned then, and smiled at him. Something akin to firecrackers went off inside his chest, and in that brief shining moment he understood that she was more than refreshing: She was necessary. Though he knew little of love and had, in fact, denied its very existence, that one simple smile proved him wrong.

The days of collecting bits and pieces of her life in a file folder were over. The days of wondering whether she was real were past. None of that mattered anymore. The only thing that mattered was that he had found her, and having found her, he was determined not to lose her.

Unfortunately he had no idea how to go about the process of wooing and winning a special woman.

"Holly?" Ben said, taking her hand. It took all his willpower not to scoop her into his arms and run. Caveman tactics. That ought to win him some points . . . as the biggest jackass this side of the Mason-Dixon line. "Do you mind if I leave you alone while I talk with the senator?"

"Not at all. This is Birmingham. I've already claimed kin to half the people in this room."

He could have kissed her. Would have if the room hadn't been full of people. But the kiss he had in mind was not for public viewing. The kiss he had in mind was the kind that melded souls as well as bodies. Though the idea of love was entirely new to him, the ways of the heart seemed natural.

He squeezed her hand, and the look he gave her was full of promise.

"Until later, then," he said.

"Later."

"She's a jewel," the senator told him as they headed toward a small sitting room across the hall from the rest of the party. "But then I guess you already know that."

"Like you said, Senator. I never miss a trick."

The senator's wife was charming, the other party guests were friendly, but they were not Ben. What was keeping him?

Holly glanced at her watch. Even if they started driving back from Birmingham that very minute, it would still be four A.M. when they got back to Tupelo.

Her feet were swollen from hours in high-heeled shoes, and if she had to smile one more time, her face was going to crack. But nobody could complain that she hadn't done her job, least of all Ben. She would relieve the tedium, he had said, and by George, that's exactly what she had done. Her friends told her she was a great raconteur, and the level of laughter that greeted her stories was ample proof.

The knowledge of her success should have made her happy, but it didn't. She wanted more. She wanted Ben to like her—more than like her. She wanted him to feel half the sparks she felt when she looked at him.

Was that asking too much? Half the sparks?

She knew that she was no raving beauty, and heaven knew her figure left a lot to be desired, but for one evening she wanted to be more than Holly Jones, social director. She wanted to be Holly Jones, desirable woman. She wanted to be Holly Jones, irresistible female. She wanted to be Holly Jones, lover, the kind of wild wanton lover who stole kisses in the dark driving home, the kind of wicked woman who drove a man so crazy, he had to stop on the side of the road and beg her to give him some relief.

Her fantasies were ridiculous, of course, especially considering that she was not at all the kind of woman a man like Ben Sullivan would marry. Marry? Shoot, she had the cart so far ahead of the horse that it would never catch up. A smart, successful big-city man like Ben would never fall in love with an average small-town woman.

When was she ever going to learn to quit chasing after impossible dreams?

"I can't imagine what's keeping them," Ginger Glenn said. "Do you want another drink?"

"No, thank you, I'll just . . ." Holly didn't remember what she was going to say, for there was Ben in the doorway, and suddenly her heart didn't know how to behave. It thumped against the hot velvet dress in such a wild and erratic way, she'd have suspected a heart attack if she weren't healthy as a horse and fairly young to boot.

"Sorry to keep you waiting, Holly," he said.

And then, miracle of miracles, he took her hand and their palms fit together perfectly.

"No problem," she said, the only problem at the moment being her ability to breathe. The last time she'd had to think how to breathe was when she'd witnessed a collision on Highway 78.

This was a collision, all right, a collision of head versus heart, of reason and fancy, of reality and dreams.

"Shall we go?" he said.

"Yes." There was no need for him to take her anywhere. He had already transported her to heaven. "Good night, Senator, Mrs. Glenn. It was so lovely to meet you."

"You, too, Holly." The senator patted her warmly on the shoulder. "Take good care of her, Ben."

Ben's smile was enigmatic. "I plan to, Senator."

FOURTEEN

How she ever got to the car was a miracle. And when she folded herself into the front seat and he took her hand, she thought she would pass out.

"You were wonderful tonight, Holly."

"Thank you." The glow that filled her lit up the car.

"You're more than welcome." He squeezed her hand. "I'm sorry I took so long with the senator."

"No need to apologize. I knew before I came that this evening was strictly business."

"It started that way."

"It started that way?"

"And then it became something else."

"Something else . . ." she whispered, hardly daring to breathe.

Was she in the wrong car? The wrong mind? The wrong body? While she wasn't looking had somebody else traded places with her? Surely this incredibly gorgeous man was not saying these things to ordinary Holly Jones.

"It's late," he said, relinquishing her hand to start the car. "You said you had made arrangements for someone to stay with your grandmother tonight, so I took the liberty of renting us rooms at the Hilton."

Rooms. More than one. Two. One for him and one for her.

She deflated as fast as a punctured balloon.

"That's fine," she said. "The drive to Tupelo is murder at night. I wouldn't want you falling asleep at the wheel."

"There's no danger of that. Not with you in the car."

"Sorry to disappoint you, but I've run out of funny stories. Maybe the radio will relieve your tedium till we get to our rooms."

She flicked the radio on. An all-night hard-rock station was the only one still playing. She hated the music that had no harmony, no words that made sense, only a heavy beat, pounding relentlessly; but anything was better than having to converse with a man who saw her as nothing more than a convenient party jokester.

"You misunderstood," he said.

"No, I didn't. You made yourself perfectly clear."

"If the idea of staying upsets you, we can go home. I can handle the drive."

"No, a hotel is fine."

"If that smile is any indication of your true feelings, I'm in trouble. You don't happen to be hiding a cache of rotten fruit in your purse, do you?"

Holly exploded with laughter. As Ben maneuvered the car through the traffic he joined in.

"I'm glad I finally broke your bad mood," he said.

"Comic relief will do it every time."

"I'll have to remember that."

Did that mean he was planning for the future, a future that included her? Fat chance, she thought, pun intended. She had managed by herself for many years, and she wasn't about to turn into the kind of woman who clung desperately to false hope. No head in the clouds for Holly Jones. Her feet were planted solidly on the ground, only sometimes she wished the ground they were planted on wasn't so lonely.

"Penny for your thoughts, Holly."

"You don't want to know."

"But I do. I want to know everything about you."

What did he want from her now? A song-and-dance routine? Wasn't her comic routine at the political rally enough?

"The details of my life would bore you to tears."

"Try me."

"I'm a small-town girl, always have been and guess I always will be."

"Is that what you want?"

"I used to long for something more, a studio apartment with lots of windows, lots of light, close enough to opera houses and art galleries so I could walk when I wanted to and listen to great music or stand in front of a Whistler or a Monet or a Renoir and drink my fill of beauty. That was after I got over the idea that I would never have a big country house with lots of kids and lots of pets and a big oak tree in the front yard so I could sit in a swing barefoot and feel the sun on my face."

Holly paused, embarrassed that she had revealed so much of herself to a man who obviously was just making polite conversation. She turned down the heater, turned down the radio, and pushed up the sleeves of her velvet dress.

"I don't know why I told you all that."

"Because I asked."

A woman with nothing to lose could be reckless.

"Why?" she said, surprised at her audacity, but pleased as well. Just because she wasn't cover-girl material didn't mean she had to be somebody's pet mouse.

He didn't answer right away. The entrance to their hotel was brightly lit, and she could see him clearly, see his hands relaxed on the steering wheel, his hair ruffled by the wind, his square jaw with a hint of dark shadow. In the closeness of the car he was both boyishly appealing and extraordinarily sensual.

He parked the car, then turned toward her.

"This is why," he said.

He reached for her and the thought that she should turn away was only fleeting. This man, this former enemy, had suddenly become the very stuff of life. It was necessary to touch him, to breathe him, to drink him in. Her skin burned and the trembling that started inside her chest shook her so hard that she had to cling to him to keep from falling, falling right out of the car and onto the cold ground.

He didn't have to say he was going to kiss her, she knew, knew by the look in his eyes, the softening of his mouth. And then that mouth was on hers, warm and moist and tender, and she was another woman, a sexy, desirable woman who knew exactly what to do with a man. Her arms went around him, and she wove her fingers through his hair. Even in the confines of the car, she and Ben were a perfect fit, a pair, together, the two of them.

Don't think about tomorrow, she told herself. *Just tonight. Only tonight.*

The kiss that was sweet beyond reason and tender beyond enduring became urgent, with hot open mouths and tongues tangled in a ritual as old as time. Holly wanted Ben as she had never wanted another man. She wanted him so badly that her skin burned with the yearning, the needing, the hunger.

His kisses told her that she was pretty, she was desirable, she was more than just somebody's grand-daughter, somebody's sister, somebody's ex-wife. If he never kissed her again, she would always be grate-ful for this moment. If he never saw her again, what he did for her tonight in the front seat of his sleek black Corvette was worth all the years of loneliness and waiting.

"I want more, Holly," he said, his voice full of quiet conviction. "I want one room and one bed."

Maybe she should have been cautious. Maybe she should have told him she didn't want to be a one-night stand. Maybe she should have questioned his motives.

But she didn't. Miracles came once in a lifetime, and she was going to reach for hers.

He took her silence for uncertainty.

"It's up to you, Holly. Whatever you say is what we will do."

She put her palm against his cheek and whispered, "One bed."

It was a king-sized bed with crisp white sheets and a green comforter, the kind of green you'd see growing on forgotten leftovers in the refrigerator. But to Holly it was the most beautiful bed in the world, for it held the promise of all the things she thought she would never have.

"Let me take your coat," Ben said.

He made even the simple act of removing her coat a sensual experience. With him pressed close behind her, she was acutely aware of his size. He towered over her, big, strong, powerful.

But his hands . . . She almost swooned when he touched her. Even through all the heavy layers of winter clothing, she felt the currents from the slow, sensuous movements of his hands. He put them on her shoulders, then ran them down the length of her arms. Briefly he intertwined his fingers with hers, and then his remarkable hands were on the move once more, sliding slowly upward until they nestled against her skin, just inside her coat collar. With one finger he drew erotic circles on her throat.

"Hmmm, that feels nice," she said.

He buried his face in her neck. "Smells nice too."

She didn't turn when he hung up her coat. The closet door opened, then closed. His footsteps made no sound on the carpet, but she knew when he came back, knew by the clean smell of his aftershave and the heat from his body that reached out and engulfed her. She was hot inside and out, burning up with the wanting of this man.

His hands were on her zipper before she realized that all the lamps in the room were on, and she would soon be standing naked in the unforgiving glare.

"Wait," she said. "The lights."

"I want to see you."

Oh, God. He would see her belly that hadn't been flat in ten years and her thighs that looked like the support posts of a stadium. Coming to this room with him had been a terrible idea. One look at her in the nude and he would change his mind. He would get a violent headache or a terrible stomachache or an instant case of hives . . . anything to keep from making love to a woman that both her exes had found unlovable.

"Maybe this is not such a good idea," she whispered.

With his hands on her shoulders, he gently turned her around. She couldn't bear to look at his face. He was a smart, worldly-wise man; he would know exactly what she was thinking.

"Holly . . . Look at me." With two fingers, he tipped up her chin. "You are charming, warm, intelligent, and fun to be with. But more than that, you are *real*."

One witty remark and she could turn this situation into something they would both laugh about on the drive back home. When she opened her mouth, he put a finger over her lips.

"Shhh, don't say anything."

He caressed her lips with slow, easy strokes that slid back and forth, back and forth, until she was so wet and wild with wanting that she nearly screamed. And when his finger dipped into her mouth and tantalized her tongue, she moaned. She couldn't help herself. Ben was the kind of man who brought out the beast in her, and she was the kind of woman who turned it loose and gave it full range.

His smile was quick, brilliant, and knowing.

"You like that, don't you?"

"Yes." More than liked it: She loved it, adored it, would walk over hot coals just for the feel of it. "You know how to drive a woman crazy, don't you?"

He seemed surprised and genuinely pleased. "Do I?"

"Ohhh, yes . . . indeed you do."

He bent over her and slid his lips down the side of her cheek, down her neck, then back up until they were close to her ear. His breath was warm against her skin.

"The feeling is mutual, Holly." He flicked his tongue into her ear. "You drive me mad."

When his mouth moved back around to capture hers, all her inhibitions tumbled away. Passion that had been dormant for so long burst into full flames, and nothing mattered except quenching the fire. Nothing mattered except the sweet torture and the aching need. Nothing mattered except the moment.

His hands were on her zipper once more, then on her shoulders, sliding downward, peeling away the clothes that hid her. She stood before him naked, the lamplight glowing in her hair and on her skin, and his eyes told her that she was beautiful. They told her that she was sexy. They told her that she was irresistible.

He caressed her, shaped her, molded her. Then his lips did the same. Everywhere he touched, she burned.

His gaze slid over her once more, and his mouth quirked upward in a rakish smile so full of raw sexual need that she went weak-kneed. He picked her up, laid her on the bed, and with exquisite care spread her hair across the pillows.

"Such beautiful hair." Strands trickled through his fingers as he watched the play of light. "It's full of fire, just like you."

She reached for him, and he came down to her, his shirt buttons pressing into her chest, his pants tweedy and warm against her bare legs. They were hungry for each other, their kisses deep and heady. Soon kissing was not enough.

Ben stripped, and before she could catch her breath over the awesome sight of him, he was holding her, his fingers exploring her where she was wet and swollen. Such expert fingers.

"That feels so good," she whispered, already writhing under his touch. "Sooo good."

"There's more where that came from. Do you want it?"

"Yes . . . I want more . . . I'm greedy, selfish, hungry . . . I want all of you."

"You'll have it, Holly, and I'll have all of you."

Warmth radiated through her, starting at the point where his fingers touched, spreading outward, spiraling upward. She felt such need, such consuming need, that she had to have more, would *die* if she didn't have more.

She told him so. Simply. Explicitly. Without guile and without embarrassment.

"You are so sexy," he whispered. "Did you know that?"

"No."

"Your ex-husbands were fools, absolute fools."

"Don't talk," she whispered, burying her face in his chest and inhaling the sexy masculine smell of him. "Love me, just love me."

Slow, sweet torture. That was the only way she could describe the way he entered her. He was huge, stretching, pulsing, filling her inch by mind-boggling inch. Impaled by him, she became a creature of pure sensation. Mindless. Liquid. Wild. Wanting.

She arched against him, encouraging him by body language to match her wantonness. But simple friction, no matter how pleasurable, was not Ben's style.

Holding his weight off her chest, he pressed his lower body flat against hers, ankle to ankle, calf to calf, thigh to thigh, groin to groin. Melded together, they began a slow, sensual tango, an erotic dance that sent Holly soaring. The climax that hit her was so intense, she cried out her surprise and pleasure.

"Good?" he whispered.

"Better than good. Magnificent. Superb. Heavenly."

"For me, too, Holly, for me too. What do you want? Tell me what you want?" he said.

But she was in a realm where logic vanished and nothing remained except feelings, pure, raw, sexual.

"I want you, just *you . . . now . . . please.*"

His face intense, his eyes so dark they appeared bottomless, Ben began a rhythm that drew all the breath from her body. About her, everything dimmed, faded until there was just Ben, only Ben and the sensations he made her feel.

There was a peak that few lovers ever reached, but she and Ben climbed it with ease, climbed to the very top, then began that tantalizing descent that sent them crashing. Holly cried out his name, clinging to his hard, sleek body lest she fall off the edge of the earth.

"I'm not finished with you yet," he said.

Ecstasy filled her . . . and a wicked impishness born of sexual freedom.

"You can't make me do that again."

"Want to bet?" The devilish gleam in his eye was matched by an equally devilish smile.

"Yes," she said, but Ben didn't need permission. Already he had begun the rhythm that resonated through every nerve in her body. Again and again she climbed the peaks. Over and over she came crashing down, each descent more intense than the one before it.

Sweat slicked their bodies and dampened her hair. It sprang into wet curls around her glowing face. Mindless, she cried out his name.

"Ben . . . Ben . . . Ben."

"I won," he said.

"I won," she whispered.

"You think it's over, do you?"

Wrapping her in a tight embrace, he tumbled off the bed. Bent at the waist, she clung to the sheets as he entered her from behind. There was no slow sweet tango this time, no gradual climb to the mountaintop, only the hard, driving force of a powerful man reaching his own climax. His sounds of pleasure were pure animal, deep, guttural, satisfied.

Holly's hands tightened on the wadded sheets as passion exploded through her. He maneuvered them back onto the bed and held her close, his breath rasping in her ear and his heart pounding against the palm of her hand.

Neither of them said anything. What they had done was beyond words.

With every lamp in the room still burning, they fell asleep in each other's arms.

FIFTEEN

It was late to be having breakfast, but Ben always started his day with the meal he termed *brain food*. The English muffins had never tasted fresher, the oranges sweeter, the milk smoother.

When he refilled his coffee cup, he stood at the window a moment appreciating the quiet beauty of the farm. Gertrude, having recovered from her misadventure at the church, was placidly munching from a mound of hay piled in the pasture. The other cows were in various states of repose, some lying under the huge oak trees, others beside the lake, while the ever-faithful Henry stood on the other side of the hay mound.

It was a tranquil scene, far removed from the hustle and bustle of Washington. Finally Ben understood why he had chosen a farm as a retreat rather than a cottage on the beach or a chalet in the mountains.

Not only could he get back to nature, but he could also be involved with nature. All he had to do was step outside his door, and he could immerse himself in the land. He could till and plow, he could sow and harvest. In dozens of ways he could be a part of the beautiful process of renewal.

"Do I detect a new jauntiness in your step, sir?" Hines asked.

"No comment," Ben said, and then he felt guilty. Hines was more than his employee: He was a staunch advocate, a best friend, a substitute father.

Coffee cup in hand, Ben turned and propped his hip on the cabinet.

"Sorry about that, Hines. Yes, I feel *great* today."

"I take it things went well on your date with Miss Jones?"

"You take it right."

"The two of you make a striking couple."

"You're jumping to conclusions, Hines. My track record with relationships is not a very good one. Celebration at this point would be premature. Besides, this is stage one. I don't know if I can handle stage two."

"I have every confidence in you, sir."

"Holly is a fine woman."

"Indeed, she is."

They drank their coffee in silence. Ben had always been certain of himself. He never questioned his motives, never questioned his actions: he merely lived in a way that advanced his career and did the least damage in the process.

Introspection was new to him. And somewhat scary.

Where did he go from here? What was he going to do about Holly?

"Hines . . ." Ben paused. He didn't know enough about relationships even to understand the questions.

"Sir?"

"I've always believed a leopard can't change his spots. Do you think it's possible?"

"I believe that anything is possible. If this leopard has a strong enough will, he can make anything happen."

Ben digested that in silence. Hines thoughtfully sipped his coffee.

"Is this leopard somebody I know, sir?"

"Yes."

"I thought so." Hines shoved his coffee cup aside and folded his hands in his lap. "Sometimes a leopard can be mistaken, sir. Sometimes he can only think he needs to change his spots, when all he needs to do is change his habits."

Ben was touched. Under the guise of watching Henry, he turned to the window and cleared his throat.

"Hines, suppose this leopard decided to change his habits. Where do you think he should start?"

"I couldn't presume to answer that. It's something the leopard will have to figure out for himself."

Expressing his feelings was new to Ben, but he had to start somewhere.

"When you go home for Christmas, I'm going to miss you. I always do. Have I ever told you that?"

"No, but I suspected as much. The feeling is mutual, sir."

If they kept up this line of conversation, the next thing Ben knew they would be sitting around bawling like two little old ladies. Come to think of it, tears might not be such a bad idea. He couldn't remember the last time he had cried.

"Well . . . Time to get to work. What did you find out about Michael Snipes?"

Hines retrieved a fat file folder from Ben's desk.

"This is not the first farm he's lost. He lived in Alabama, Georgia, and Arkansas before coming to Mississippi. He kept his farm in Alabama two years, then the year they lived in Georgia he worked as a night watchman, a school custodian, and a security guard. In Arkansas he mostly drew unemployment."

"Bottom line?"

"He's a ne'er-do-well, sir."

And Holly's friend.

Ben's brow furrowed as he studied the folder. There was more. Jo Ann Snipes had tried to attend night school, but each time she had to drop out because Michael was moving on. The children's grades had suffered because of moving from school to school.

Ben had never subscribed to the theory that throwing money at a problem was the way to solve it. There had to be another way. When he lived in D.C., he took long walks along Pennsylvania Avenue when he needed to wrestle with a problem. Now he had the farm.

"I'm going for a walk, Hines. When I get back, we'll talk."

Ben grabbed his jacket from a hook on the back porch. He'd been so busy moving then doing repairs that he had never taken the time to walk his land. The wind was bracing, the fallen leaves crisp under his feet, the Mississippi sun bright and warmer than it should have been for December. By the time Ben reached the curve in the path that led to the lake, he shed his coat.

Henry looked up at his passing and brayed a greeting. Maybe the jackass was getting to like him. Maybe Ben was getting to like himself.

The water was still and peaceful, and while Ben stood at its edge a blue crane swooped in for a landing. Standing in the water on its long skinny legs, it was both awkward and graceful. As Ben watched it the solution to his problem presented itself. That's the way it usually happened: While his conscious mind thought of something else, his unconscious mind was busy solving the problem.

He hurried back to the house and told Hines his plan.

"That's brilliant, sir. And very generous, might I add."

"You understand all the stipulations?"

"I do."

"There's one more. Holly is never to know."

Growing up unloved and unwanted, Ben had learned the hard way that it was impossible to buy affection. Nor did he want Holly to think that he was trying. Love, if it ever came to him, had to come freely.

For two days after she returned from Birmingham, Holly walked with a new spring in her step. She sang along with every song on the radio, whether or not she knew the words. She dragged every box of Christmas decorations she had into the living room and hung them all. Lily complained that the house looked like a garage sale, but even she couldn't dampen Holly's spirits.

Every time the phone rang, she raced to answer it. And every time it wasn't Ben, her spirits sank.

On the third day the phone call was from Jo Ann Snipes.

"Holly, can you take a break this afternoon and meet me for coffee?"

"Sure. I can always make the time for you, Jo Ann."

They met at a homey restaurant on the corner of Main and Spring. Jo Ann was already waiting with two cups of coffee when Holly slid into the booth.

"What's wrong?" Holly said.

"How often have you asked me that question in the past year?"

"More times than I care to think about. What is it, Jo Ann? You look shaken."

"I am. Incredible news sometimes does that." She gave Holly a huge smile.

"Incredible news? As in *good* news?" Holly reached for her friend's hands. "Don't keep me guessing. What is it?"

"You're not going to believe this. I don't believe it, myself."

"What? *What?*"

"Michael got a call from a lawyer, somebody he'd never heard of. Holly . . . somebody *paid off our mortgage!*"

"Who?"

"If I knew, I'd fall on the ground and kiss his feet."

"Or hers," Holly said. "It could be a woman."

"Nope. The lawyer said *he* prefers to remain anonymous."

"Whoever he is, here's to him." Holly lifted her coffee cup. "May peace, love, and all the joy of Christmas be his."

"Amen." Jo Ann touched the rim of Holly's cup with her own.

"There's more, Holly."

"You're driving me crazy with all this suspense. Tell me, quick."

"This donor, bless his dear and generous heart, provided us a nest egg to make a fresh start. He also provided a small monthly stipend for one year with the stipulation that I go back to school and that Michael get a job and remain there for that period of time."

"That's wonderful, Jo Ann. I'm thrilled for you." Holly loved a good mystery. But more than that, she loved solving it. "It must be someone you know. Think, Jo Ann. Who could it be?"

"I've racked my brain, but the only person I can think of who would do such a thing is you."

Holly laughed. "When my ship comes in . . . Hey, maybe it's some long-forgotten relative."

"Fat chance. But enough about me. What about you?"

"Same old same old," Holly said, but immediately she felt guilty. "That's not entirely true, Jo Ann. I don't know how to tell you this. I feel somewhat like a traitor."

"You! Never. You're the best friend I've got."

"I hope you still think so after I tell you. I had a date with Ben Sullivan. I really like him, Jo Ann."

"Oh, Holly. Sure, we laughed and joked about him stealing the farm, but I never blamed him. Losing the farm was our own doing, but now we're getting a second chance. I'm glad you are too."

"Make that a *third* chance. I'm scared to death, Jo Ann."

"You're the most intrepid person I know, Holly. If anybody can make this work, you can."

Holly didn't have the heart to tell Jo Ann that she wasn't intrepid at all. The jokes, the laughter, the happy-go-lucky smile were all part of an act designed to cover her own fears and insecurities. She had failed to live up to her potential. She had failed at two marriages.

Shoot. Ben Sullivan hadn't even called her. It looked as if she wasn't even going to get up to bat a third time, let alone fail to hit a home run.

SIXTEEN

The church kitchen smelled deliciously spicy. Pans of gingerbread boys were cooling on the racks while the last of the batch was baking in the oven.

"I'll be glad to get home and get my feet up," Loweva grumbled. "Whoever heard of having a party at the church this close to Christmas? That's family time."

"It'll be fun, Loweva. Besides, some of these people don't have family." Holly pulled out tubes of icing and set to work.

"Lordy, what're you doing to the gingerbread?"

"Turning pretty boys into sweet jolly Santas. I wish it was this easy in real life."

"Is that pretty boy giving you trouble?"

Holly didn't even think of pretending with Loweva. "Ben hasn't called since Birmingham."

"I know what you're thinking, and that's plain foolish. There's nothing wrong with you."

"I'm fat."

"You're not fat; you've got a little meat on your bones. There's a difference."

"To you, maybe, but not to him. He's gorgeous. Why would he want a woman with thunder thighs and a jelly roll around the middle when he could have anybody he wanted? I was a one-night stand, that's all."

"You don't know that."

"Then why hasn't he called?"

"Maybe he has his reasons."

"What reasons?"

"Why don't you ask him?"

"How? I'm not about to be the first to call, and I'm certainly not going to drive out to the farm."

Loweva smiled. "All you have to do is turn around. Yonder he is. Hmm-hmmm, he is one *fine-*looking man."

With a tube of icing in one hand and a gingerbread boy in the other, Holly whirled around. And there he was, standing in the doorway, taking her breath away. Looking at him that way, relaxed, smiling, his jeans pressed just so, his stark white shirt relieved by a flamboyant tie of red and green, Holly remembered all the ways he had touched her, all the things he had made her feel. In Ben's arms she felt loved and secure and cared for. She felt intelligent and appreciated. She felt pretty.

She was mad at him for giving her those things and then taking them away. No matter how appealing he was, that didn't make up for putting her through four days of silent hell.

Maybe she wasn't *Vogue* material, maybe she wasn't Ph.D material, but by George, she was *somebody*, and she deserved to be treated that way. And she was going to march over there and tell him so.

"What will I say to him, Loweva?" she whispered, turning back to her gingerbread boys.

"Who do you think I am? Dear Abby? Even if I was I couldn't get up a bunch of advice in this length of time. He's headed this way."

"Shoot." Holly squeezed the tube too hard and a glob of red icing plopped onto the top of the worktable. The resolute sound of Ben Sullivan's footsteps reminded her that he was coming closer.

"My goodness . . . my hair. I look like a squirrel."

Between doing Lily's errands and getting ready for the church party, she hadn't even had time to shampoo it. She'd bunched it high on her head in a rubber band, and then added a bit of mistletoe and some jingle bells for a festive touch.

"You talk to him, Loweva. I'm busy."

"All right, I will."

Loweva grabbed a tray of cups and headed Ben's way.

"I sure am glad you came early," she said. "We could use some help back there in the kitchen."

Another glob of red icing went astray. Holly could have killed her.

"It will be my pleasure," Ben said. "Just tell me what to do."

"Ask Holly. She's the boss."

Holly didn't have to turn around and look through the serving window to see Ben headed her way. She could feel his presence.

"Where's the angel costume?" He leaned casually on the edge of the worktable as if he were an old hand in her kitchen instead of making his second appearance, as if she were merely the cook and Birmingham had never happened.

"An angel costume wouldn't be appropriate." She bared her teeth at him. "A devil would suit me better tonight."

"Is anything wrong?"

"Is anything *wrong*?" She aimed the icing gun at him, tempted to shoot. "Now, why in the world would anything be wrong?"

His puzzlement looked genuine, but she didn't care. Wounded pride did that to women, made them spit and claw like cornered cats.

"You tell me," he said.

"I'm getting ready for a large party," she said.

"I heard. That's why I'm here."

She bristled. "I see."

Ben shoved his hands into his pockets.

"I'm not very good at this."

That's what he had told Jonathan. *I'm not a joiner. I don't believe in institutions . . . of any kind.*

Including the age-old institution of courtship, obviously. Or else he would have called.

Her hands shook as she wielded the icing gun over the rest of the gingerbread. It didn't help her mood any that Ben looked cool and collected. It didn't improve her attitude one bit that she found him desirable even when she was furious at him.

Why didn't he say something? This was probably the way he dealt with opponents in Washington, treated them to an overdose of his devastatingly good looks while he stood silently by and watched them sweat.

She snatched up her pan of gingerbread. "Would you mind moving your . . ." Her eyes raked over his chest, down his flat belly, to the part of his anatomy she had in mind. The memory of touching him there rendered her speechless.

"Moving my *what*?" His voice was softly seductive.

She licked her lips. "Hips," she said.

As he complied his smile was one of pure wicked glee. "Certainly. Is that far enough?"

Holly had been done in by too many gorgeous men to let one more get the best of her.

"No," she said, tossing her head. "But I suppose I can make do."

Head high, she stalked by him and placed the pan of freshly baked gingerbread on the serving counter. Out in the Fellowship Hall, Loweva grinned at her. Holly made a slashing motion across her throat. Loweva only laughed.

Ben was still in her kitchen, too big to be overlooked and too powerful to be ignored. Clutching the edge of the counter, Holly considered what to do next.

Ask him, Loweva had said. But she had too much pride. Asking why he hadn't called would be like begging. And she wasn't about to beg for a man's attentions.

But she couldn't stand idle all night. Soon the Fellowship Hall would contain fifty people who had no other place to go on Christmas Eve, fifty people who for one reason or another wouldn't be in the bosom of a loving family.

What about Ben? Why was he there?

To drive her crazy. That was why.

She whirled around, intent on stalking by him once more, but his hand snaked out and snared her wrist.

"Holly, I came to see you."

If the shocking currents moving through her weren't enough to keep her still, the grip on her wrist was. But could she believe what he said? Did she dare believe?

"Why?" she said.

"Hines is with his family in Virginia, and for some reason I didn't want to be alone. The newsletter I received said this was a Christmas party for strays." His eyes sought hers.

"I see," she said.

"No, you don't, because I haven't told you the whole truth. But this is neither the time nor the place for it."

Whatever the truth was, it would have to wait.

The door opened to let in a blast of cold and the first of Holly's strays. Cheery greetings filled the fellowship hall.

"I have to go and see to the guests," she said. And then, because he looked so lost and sincere, Holly relented. "I'm glad you came," she said, simply and truthfully.

"You mean that, don't you?"

"Yes."

"I was hoping that after the party is over, you could come to the farm to help decorate my tree."

Holly loved decorating Christmas trees. To her, it was an intensely personal chore, one that ensured warmth and invited reminiscing. Decorating a tree together was intimate in ways that even making love was not.

She wished she could join him with the full assurance that it meant the same thing to him, but she'd had her hopes built up too many times to see them dashed once more.

"Lily is home by herself," she said, which was true. "I don't like to leave her alone on Christmas Eve." Also true. The main reason she didn't want to go to the farm was self-protection. She didn't know how many times a woman could pick up the pieces of herself and go on about her business, but Holly figured she was getting close to her limit.

"I understand," Ben said, and if he was disappointed, she couldn't tell.

The crowd in the Fellowship Hall was growing and would soon demand all Holly's attention.

"Thank you, anyway," she said.

"If you change your mind, I'll be there." She turned to leave, but his compelling voice called her back. "Holly . . . I hope you do."

His voice held her, and his dark eyes made her remember the way he had touched her, the way he had held her, the way he had made love to her. She wanted so much to believe that he was sincere. She wanted desperately to believe that she was not disposable to him.

But duty called and she had a legitimate excuse to leave him, a valid reason to avoid the kind of soul-searching she wasn't ready to do.

"Gotta go," she said. Then she did what she had been doing for years: She gave him a big grin and cheerful wave. "Merry Christmas, Ben. Enjoy the party."

She didn't know whether he did or not. With Ben it was impossible to tell what he was thinking. At least he stayed. That was progress. Maybe.

Jonathan and his family took time from their own celebration to come to the church party. Ben joined them. He ate with them, talked with them, and only occasionally did his eyes seek out Holly.

By the time the party was over, she was exhausted from all the tension, all the uncertainty.

"Go on home to your family, Loweva," she said after the last guest had gone. "I'll finish here."

"I'm not fixing to leave you to clean up all this mess by yourself."

"But it's Christmas, Loweva."

"Last I heard, it was Christmas at your house too. If Grover and the kids know what's good for 'em, they'll wait for me."

They had deliberately kept the party short and simple, and there wasn't much cleaning up to do. They worked in silence for a while, which was unusual for them.

"I take it my little plan didn't work," Loweva said. Holly didn't have to inquire which plan. Nor did she feel obligated to answer. The question was purely rhetorical.

"If you want to talk about it, I've got big ears and plenty of time."

"What is there to say, Loweva?"

"You didn't talk about *anything* with him?"

"Nothing that couldn't be put in a newsletter for the whole congregation to read."

"Hmmm-hmmm." Loweva shook her head. "Honey, I don't know what I'm gonna do with you."

"He invited me over to decorate his tree."

"What did you tell him?"

"I told him no. Don't look at me like that, Loweva. You know good and well I have to spend the evening with Lily."

"She goes to bed at nine. What about after?"

"It's not a good idea."

"I guess not, seeing as how you've already made up your mind that he's like the two sorry so-and-sos you married. He seems mighty different to me, but who am I to judge? I'm just a uneducated woman been married to the same good man for forty years.

No need to ask a woman like me about love. Hmmm-hmmm. Nosirree."

Holly threw the last of the paper plates into the garbage, then untied her apron and pulled off her rubber gloves. As she stashed them in a drawer her shoulders drooped.

"Come here, honey." Loweva put her arms around Holly and swayed in a gentle rocking rhythm. "Sometimes old Loweva's bad to the bone. You don't have to have no man to make you feel good about yourself. You got me. I'm ugly and mean, but it's all right by me if you don't want nothing else."

"I'm scared," Holly said, her voice muffled against Loweva's ample shoulder. "It's not because of the way he looks and the way I look. That's just an excuse."

Loweva patted her shoulders. "Hush now. It's Christmas Eve. I'm sorry I started all this talk."

Holly lifted her head and looked into Loweva's kind face.

"I'm in love with him, and I'm scared that he won't love me back. Loweva, what if he won't love me back?"

SEVENTEEN

Ben was not accustomed to failure. The fact that Holly turned down his invitation stung. In Washington, everything had come with ease—lobbying, making money, socializing both for business and pleasure.

Alone on the farm with his naked tree, he felt foolish. And lonely.

He was glad that Hines had a family to go home to every Christmas, but in the past Ben had been in a big city where any number of people and parties were only a cab drive away. He had never had to endure Christmas in the wilderness, as Hines called it. Now Ben knew why. He had never felt such absolute stillness, heard such absolute silence. The house echoed with it.

And the tree . . . Hines had meant well. He had meant to bring a homey touch to Ben's Christmas, but the opposite was true. The tree reminded Ben of all the things he had never had—pictures of the family opening gifts together and posing around the tree and sledding in the snow; ornaments that would be passed on from generation to generation, some made of tacky construction paper at school, others created in the kitchen with saltwater dough and children's paints and lots of love.

He didn't have any ornaments, let alone the kind that would be treasured by kids and grandkids. Not that he was close to having any. At the rate he was going, he would be a bachelor the rest of his life. But not by choice. No longer by choice.

The bare branches of the tree looked pathetic, and the Christmas CD he'd put on the player sounded mournful. Ben switched it off. No use setting the stage for Christmas cheer. No use setting the stage for anything. It was after eleven. Holly was not coming.

Tomorrow he would take the tree back into the woods and replant it. Or he might just throw it out the door. Why bother trying to change his ways?

Without a backward glance at the tree, he strode to his desk. It was there, his Christmas gift to Holly. He was glad now that he hadn't wrapped it and put it under the tree. Bad enough that he had to see it every time he opened the drawer. Under the tree, wrapped in silver and tied with a red ribbon, it would have been torture.

He was closing the desk drawer when he heard the car. His hand froze. Fighting the temptation to look out the window, he sat down in one of the leather wing chairs and waited.

No use getting excited. It could be a neighbor looking for a lost cow.

The knock was soft, tentative. He could see her silhouette through the glass in the door. Her hair was loose, the way he liked it. The glow from the bulb gave her a halo.

"I hope it's not too late," she said when he opened the door.

"No, of course not. Come in."

He stood back and held the door open for her. His heart was hammering so hard, he could hardly speak.

"I guess I should have called first."

He gave a negative shake of his head. What to say? What to do? He felt foolish and awkward. If this was what caring deeply for another person felt like all the time, he wasn't sure he wanted to care.

But love was not that simple. He couldn't change his mind, for his heart was in charge.

"I was afraid if I called, you would have changed your mind, and then I thought that I might change mine, and so I waited until after Lily and I had dinner and opened our gifts and she was in bed. . . ."

Holly lifted her gaze to his, and he wanted to take her in his arms right then and forget about the tree, forget about the courtship, forget about saying and doing the proper thing. He wanted her. It was that simple—and that scary.

Holly must have read his thoughts. She drew a sharp breath and caught her lower lip between her teeth.

"What if she wakes up? I left her a note, but she might wake up and not see it, and then she would panic and maybe fall and hurt herself. . . ." She turned toward the door. "I have to go back."

"Holly . . ." He didn't reach out and hold her back. If she stayed, it had to be of her own free will. "Don't go."

She was slow turning back to him, and when she did, her eyes were so warm and wide and blue, he thought he knew what heaven must look like.

"Why?" she whispered.

"Because Birmingham meant something to me."

She regarded him solemnly for so long that he was afraid he had said the wrong thing, afraid he had scared her off. What would he do if she turned away from him? After waiting so long to find her, losing her would be unbearable.

"Do you really mean that?" she said.

"Yes." Where was all his glibness when he needed it?

"When you didn't call, I didn't know what to think."

"I had some business matters to take care of." And then, because she looked uncertain, he offered more explanation. "I focus on one thing at a time, Holly. When it's business, I'm all business." He shrugged, smiling. "I guess that has always been my focus . . . until now."

"I was so afraid to come here tonight."

"Why?"

"I'm afraid of caring too much. I'm afraid of being

disposable. I can't bear it if you think of me as disposable."

"You are many things, Holly. Disposable is not
one of them." She still stood apart from him, wearing
her coat, as if she might flee at any minute.

He had the perfect opening to say all the things
on his heart. *I love you.* Only three words. Why
couldn't he say them?

"Let me take your coat," he said, and then without waiting for her reply he slid it off her shoulders
and hung it in his closet.

So, he was a coward. But after all, he was new at
this. He needed more time, that was all.

Her coat smelled faintly of ginger lily. He resisted
the urge to bury his face in the soft wool. Instead he
caressed the collar as he hung it up. It looked good
hanging next to his blue windbreaker and his tweed
topcoat. He shoved the hangers close enough so that
their coats were touching.

"Is that the tree?" Holly said, rubbing her arms.

"Are you cold? I can add another log to the fire."

"That would be nice."

He was reluctant to leave her, even for a moment.
As soon as he was out of sight, he sprinted. Across the
back porch, out the door, to the woodpile, then back
again. In the kitchen he slowed down to catch his
breath.

What would Hines say if he could see Ben now?
He chuckled thinking about it. He was still grinning
when he joined Holly in the den.

"What's funny?" she said, smiling back at him.

"Life."

"I noticed you dug the tree instead of chopping it down," she said.

"I'll replant it after Christmas."

"I'm glad."

It had been Hines's idea, but Ben took the credit. He needed all the points with Holly he could get, and besides, Hines would approve if he were there. Ben would tell him about it tomorrow when he called.

Ben squatted beside the fireplace, then arranged the wood and tended it until the fresh logs caught and cast their warmth through the room. Holly came to stand beside the blaze, her skirt swishing in a manner uniquely feminine and extremely sensual.

He stood beside her, her skirt brushing his leg, her shoulder touching his. It was a cozy intimacy enhanced by the glow of the fire and the sound of the winter wind in the eaves. It was the kind of intimacy that invited touching. Ben reached for Holly's hand.

"I'm really glad you came."

"I can't stay long," she said, "just long enough to help you decorate the tree. I suppose you have balls."

"Yes, but I don't plan to hang them on a tree."

A lively pink colored her cheeks, but she chuckled. That was one of the things he enjoyed about Holly—her ability to laugh at herself.

"Sorry about that," he said. "I couldn't resist."

"That's okay. They say laughter is the best medicine."

"For what?"

"Everything, I guess."

He turned her hand over and studied the palm, then because it was soft and pink and vulnerable looking, he bent over and kissed it. The shiver that ran through her made him feel like a hero. Such a simple thing, that kiss. And yet Holly's reaction told him that she felt the sparks too.

What had she said to him earlier? *I don't want to be disposable.* Two men had cast her aside as if she were a worn-out pair of shoes. Ben would never do that to her. And yet he wasn't ready to say words that had always scared the hell out of him. He wasn't ready to commit himself to an institution whose statistics proved it to be a bad risk.

"I'm not good at this, Holly."

She didn't play coy with him. She didn't widen her eyes and pretend not to know what he was talking about.

"I'm not either," she said.

"I don't want you to think that I lured you out here merely for sex—though, God knows I want you."

"During that long silence, I thought you didn't."

Ben caught her face in his hands and tilted it upward. "I don't want you ever to think that, Holly. Not ever."

Her lips looked soft and inviting when she smiled, and Ben leaned down for a taste. They were as sweet as he remembered, and then some. The animal didn't want the kiss to end there, but the man who was struggling with emotions that were new and strange understood that sex would camouflage other feelings that were important in the growth of a relationship.

"How about that tree?" he said when he released her.

"Bring on the decorations. I'm ready."

Ben fetched lights and tinsel and three boxes of ornaments he'd picked up at the local discount store. Nothing fancy, just ordinary cheap glass Christmas balls in red and green and gold.

"I'm not so sure you would want my help if you could see our tree," Holly said. "Lily saved every ornament James and I made, no matter how tacky they were. We have construction-paper angels with lopsided halos, bread-dough Santas that the mice have chewed on, fake stained-glass windows, the kind you make from a kit, all green. Picasso had his Blue Period; I had my green one. Oh, and you should see the treetop angel. She's bald. I made her a wig last year, but it got lost in the shuffle."

He loved the animation on her face as she reminisced. He loved hearing about her childhood that was so vastly different from his. Even if he did peg Lily as someone who wasn't good for Holly's self-esteem, he was glad to know that she had some redeeming qualities.

"I can't wait to see your ornaments." Her face fell when she saw the boxes from Wal-Mart. "Of course, not everybody is as sentimental as I am."

"Not everybody had a childhood worthy of tucking away keepsakes."

She touched his hand, softly. "I'm so sorry, Ben. I would never have carried on like that if I had known."

He didn't want her pity.

"No problem, Holly. I'm learning that there are a few decent people in this world who are what they seem to be, but there are as many bad ones who don't know the meaning of kindness and decency, let alone love. They are somebody's sons and daughters, fathers and mothers, brothers and sisters. A couple of them happen to belong in my family. It's the luck of the draw."

"I accepted it a long time ago." He smiled, hoping to restore her cheerful mood. "Now, tell me what goes on first."

"The lights."

He strung the lights and together they hung the Christmas ornaments and the tinsel. Holly was easy to be with, full of uninhibited laughter and high spirits. She collected anecdotes with the same enthusiasm that she collected mementos of her past.

"Tell me about Washington," she said, after regaling him with several funny stories gleaned from years of working in the church's kitchen.

"There's nothing much to tell. I did my job and they paid me well."

Ben hung the last ornament, and they stood back to view the tree. It looked like something you would see in the display window of a department store, bright, colorful, and as impersonal as the smile of a salesclerk.

Holly's hand stole into his.

"If you don't mind getting your hands dirty, I still remember the recipe for bread-dough ornaments."

Here was a woman with enough warmth and generosity for two. Loving such a woman carried all kinds of possibilities.

Long ago he had given up the hope of having the kind of life that created precious memories—celebrating birthdays and sharing Christmases, holding hands in the car and stealing a kiss when the light turned red, eating from the same box of popcorn at movies and laughing at silly jokes that weren't funny to anybody except them. Holly was his one chance to have all that, and more. So much more.

All he had to do was reach out.

But what if it was too soon? What if he did it wrong? What if she said no?

"This could get messy," Holly said. "Are you sure you want to do this?"

It was a small step, making a Christmas memory with Holly. But at least it was a start.

"Sure," he said. "Lead the way."

In the kitchen Holly showed him how to mix the dough, and they laughed when he got more flour on himself than in the bowl. They made Santas and unicorns and angels, all with blue eyes and red hair because Ben insisted they should look like Holly.

It was after midnight when the bread-dough ornaments were ready to hang.

"You hang the first one because it's your house and your tree," she said. "Choose one."

He chose an angel. How could he do otherwise?

When the last ornament was hung, Holly turned to smile at him, and it seemed natural to put his arms around her. She leaned her head on his shoulder, and he caressed her hair.

"I want you, Holly," he said.

"Yes."

That was all she said, all she needed to say. They made slow, sweet love in front of the blazing fire in a room that finally looked and felt like a real home.

They slept for a while, then the fire died down and the chill woke them up.

"Cold?" Ben pulled Holly closer.

"Hmmm. I'm never cold with you. You're like a heater. I wonder what your body temperature is."

His chuckle was deep and sexy. "Hotter when you're around."

He kissed the side of her mouth, the lobe of her ear, the soft vulnerable spot at the base of her neck. It astonished him how much he wanted this woman. Though it had been only hours since they made love, his need for her was urgent and strong. She excited him in a way no woman ever had.

"Don't move," he told her. Then he added another log to the fire and stretched full length in front of it, naked and unashamed, the evidence of his need on full display.

The firelight turned her hair to flame as she bent over him. She was as bold as he, taking him deep into her mouth, her eyes seeking his so she could see the pleasure she gave him.

"You are so good," he said, weaving his hands

through her hair and guiding her closer. "So very good."

The bulbs on the Christmas tree were still on, and their faint glow, coupled with the glow of the fire, provided the only light in the room. It was Christmas Day, the first one Ben ever remembered waking up to with joy and a sense of wonder. He knew his contentment had nothing to do with time and place, but everything to do with the woman who still knelt over him.

He stroked her hair, then released it and watched as it fanned across his belly. With the languid movements of a sensual woman, she shifted, then wrapped her hair around his rigid shaft, winding it slowly and softly until he was encased in silk and flame.

"Whatever you're doing, don't stop."

"I'm wrapping a gift," she said. "Merry Christmas, Ben."

"It is, isn't it?"

Smiling, he unwrapped the gift and gave it back to her. Her cries of pleasure were his reward.

EIGHTEEN

It was almost daylight when Holly let herself through her front door. If she were lucky, Lily would still be sleeping, and she could slip into bed undetected.

Christmas Day. And what a beautiful gift Ben had given her. The most miraculous gift she could ever hope to receive. While he hadn't said the words she longed to hear, he had shown her in a hundred different ways that he cared. Her lips curved into a satisfied smile as she remembered all those ways. She was still smiling when she walked into her den.

"Oh, my heavens," Lily said into the receiver. Dressed in gown and robe, she was sitting on the sofa with the phone in one hand and the telephone book open on her lap. "Holly just walked in the door."

There were indistinct sounds on the other end of the line, then Lily thrust the receiver at Holly.

"James wants to talk to you."

The color drained from Holly's face and her legs went weak.

"Has something happened?" she asked Lily.

"James wants to talk." Lily closed the telephone book and pulled the wool afghan off the back of the sofa and over her legs.

Suddenly all of Holly's energy drained. She wanted to sit down but decided against it. It was never a good idea to be too relaxed when she talked to her brother.

"James, what's wrong?"

"You tell me."

"What is that supposed to mean?"

"Lily calls at the crack of dawn to say that you've disappeared."

"Disappeared? James, I was visiting a friend. I left her a note."

"You went off without telling her and left her a note? What kind of way is that to look after Lily? For God's sake, Holly, she's nearly eighty years old."

"I realize that. She's not an invalid, you know. She's perfectly healthy and amazingly spry for her age."

"My arthritis is killing me," Lily interjected. "And my feet are cold. Tell James how cold my feet get in this drafty house."

"That doesn't excuse what you did, Holly," James was saying. "She was worried sick about you. She was going to call the police. Thank God she called me first. I don't know what she would have done if I hadn't been here."

Why aren't you here now? Holly wanted to scream. *She's your grandmother too.*

Her head was beginning to ache. Rubbing her forehead, Holly sank onto a blue chintz ottoman.

She had never said anything like that to her brother, and she wouldn't today, not with Lily in the same room. Holly loved her grandmother too much to say anything that would make her feel unwanted. She didn't resent being the one to take care of Lily, though sometimes Holly wished she had the freedom to come and go as she pleased without having to worry that the elderly woman might get cold or get sick or panic.

After the holidays she might drive up to Memphis and have a talk with James. Perhaps he and Gwen could let Lily stay with them for a few weeks. Even a few days would be a blessing.

"What if something had happened to her, Holly?" James was saying.

"It didn't, James. She's okay."

"No thanks to you. I swear, Holly, sometimes I don't know what's going to become of you."

"What do you mean by that? I'm healthy and happy. I have lots of great friends, and I make my own living. Just because I don't perform to your standards doesn't mean that I'm a failure."

"I didn't say you were, Holly, but you have to admit that you've made some pretty bad choices."

Holly didn't want to talk about her past. It was over and done with. She had learned a few lessons, but she had no intention of wallowing in guilt and self-pity just because she'd learned them the hard way.

"It's Christmas, James . . . Merry Christmas."

"Same to you, Holly."

"Are you and Gwen and the kids coming down today? I'd like to see you, and I know Lily would love it."

"Can't make it. Gwen's parents are coming over for lunch."

"How about this afternoon? You drive down and be back before night. Or Lily and I could drive up."

"That's not a good idea, Holly. Gwen and I promised the children we'd take them to a movie this afternoon. A family outing, you know. We don't get to have those very often."

Though he was only an hour and a half away, they hadn't seen James for the last five years at Christmastime. It was perfectly obvious that they weren't going to see him this year either. But Holly persisted anyway. She might have told herself that she was doing it because of Lily, if she hadn't known better. Sure, her motives were partly noble, but his remark about her bad choices still stung. Holly was not a plaster saint: She was out for revenge.

"How about tomorrow?" she said. "The tree will still be up, and we can postpone unwrapping the gifts until then."

"I have to be back at work."

"The day after Christmas?"

"How do you think I got where I am today,

Holly? A firm the size of mine doesn't run itself, you know."

"Yes, I know. Are Kenneth and Michelle up? I'd like to tell them Merry Christmas, and I'm sure Grandma would love to speak to them."

"They've been up since the crack of dawn. Couldn't wait to see whether Santa brought all the loot they'd ordered. Let me see if I can round them up."

His footsteps echoed on the polished parquet floor, and then there was an echoing silence as James went downstairs to fetch his children.

"Hi, Aunt Holly." It was Kenneth's excited voice. "Guess what Santa brought me."

"A quarter for your front tooth?"

"Aunt *Holly* . . . that's the tooth fairy."

Kenneth launched into a long narrative about his gifts, then his sister came on the line. After both Holly and Lily had talked to the children, Lily cast aside her afghan and went into the kitchen to make coffee.

"I can do that," Holly said.

"No, you have to cook the turkey and make the dressing. Not too much sage. James doesn't like sage."

"I thought I would do something different this year, Lily. Maybe pork loin and a nice green salad."

"But that won't be enough. Growing children need plenty of food." Her hands shook as she measured coffee into the filter.

"Lily . . ." Holly took the measuring spoon and

finished the job. "James and his family won't be here today, but Jo Ann and Michael Snipes are coming over. You'll enjoy the children."

"Poor James, always so busy. We'll have to make some of that good fudge and send him a big box. Do we have any pecans?"

"Yes, we have pecans."

"Good. James likes lots of pecans."

"Lily, did you hear me say that the Snipes family is coming?"

"I heard. I'm not deaf, you know."

Lily rummaged in the cabinets until she found the pecans. She stood uncertainly, holding on to the bag, her lips trembling. From under his cage cover Popeye called out for help. Lily put the pecans back in the cabinet and shut the door.

"Let's forget about that candy," she said. "Do we have any fresh lemons?"

"Yes. Why?"

"I thought I'd make a lemon icebox pie."

It was Holly's favorite dessert. When she was growing up, Lily had made her a lemon icebox pie to celebrate every important occasion—Holly's birthday, the first A she made in school, the day she won the spelling bee.

The scent of baby powder tickled Holly's nose as she held Lily close. Every morning when Lily dressed, she turned her clothes wrong side out, laid them on the bed, and dusted them with baby powder.

Until today Holly hadn't realized how closely she associated that scent with her grandmother.

"Thank you, Grandma," she said.

"Hmmph. No need to thank me yet. You haven't tasted it."

The Snipeses arrived in time to help set the table. There was much cause for celebration at that Christmas Day meal, for Michael had a job as night watchman at the local tire plant. Not only that but he had found a small country house on a five-acre lot.

"We can have animals again," Timmy said.

After lunch the children and Michael visited with Lily while Jo Ann and Holly cleared the table.

"I'm going back to school, Holly. I thought I'd start small, maybe take only one course the spring semester till I get used to it." She laughed. "I can tell the children exactly how they ought to study, but I'm not sure I know how myself."

"You'll get the hang of it. I'm so proud of you, Jo Ann. Nobody deserves happiness more than you."

Jo Ann started to say something, then busied herself with the dishes.

"What?" Holly asked.

"It's just . . . oh, nothing."

"Jo *Ann*, come on. You know I can't stand that kind of suspense."

"This is probably something that you already know."

"*What?*"

"I found out who our anonymous benefactor is—Ben Sullivan."

"Ben?" Holly almost dropped the plate she was holding. "Are you sure?"

"You didn't know? He hasn't told you?"

"No, Ben has never mentioned it. As terrible as I've been to him about taking your farm, wouldn't you think he would tell me? Why didn't he tell me?"

"I'm sorry. I never should have mentioned it."

"No, I'm glad you did. It just goes to show . . ."

Holly didn't know what it showed about the man. Did it mean that Ben kept secrets? Perhaps he knew she would find out, and it meant that he was trying to get on her good side.

But why? He was already there.

Maybe it meant that he was like James. Maybe Ben thought she didn't have enough intelligence to understand the significance of anything involving business.

Jo Ann put her hand on Holly's arm. "Please don't let this change whatever is going on between the two of you. You're the best friend I've ever had. I wouldn't want to be the cause of spoiling things for you."

"Are you absolutely positive it was Ben?"

"When I went to pick up the check, the regular girl was out sick and somebody else was filling in. She let it slip."

"How?"

"She asked if Mr. Sullivan was family or just a friend. I told her just a friend."

Just a friend. And a very wealthy friend at that. Holly was struck by a terrible thought. What if Ben had kept the secret from her because he thought she was a gold digger?

It made perfect sense. Ben had never said he loved her, let alone that he wanted to marry her. All he had said was that he wanted her.

She was merely his playmate. It didn't matter if playmates were gold diggers—as long as they were willing to play.

Could she settle for that?

NINETEEN

Holly's Christmas gift was still in the his desk drawer where Ben had left it. He opened the drawer for the tenth time and looked at it. He had intended to give it to her the previous night when she was there, but first they had made ornaments and they had decorated the tree and then they had settled in beside the fire and nothing else had mattered.

He had gotten sidetracked. That was all.

So, what was holding him back today? He didn't like to think about it.

He closed the desk drawer and picked up the telephone. Hines answered on the first ring.

"Were you sitting beside the telephone waiting for my call?" Ben said.

The idea pleased him. As far as he knew, Hines was the only one who ever did that.

"It *is* Christmas Day, sir."

"So it is. How's the family?"

"Noisy."

"You miss me, do you?"

"That might be stretching it a bit, sir, but I do miss the peace and quiet of the farm. I think I'm turning into a recluse."

"Then it would suit you to have the farm all to yourself for a while?"

"Have the farm to myself? Have you made some plans that I should know about?"

"I thought I might head up to D.C. and help Senator Glenn out with his farm bill."

"You're moving back?"

"No. I've come to enjoy the simple lifestyle too much to chuck it and get back into that rat race. I thought it might be good to keep my hand on the political pulse."

"Good idea, sir. No need to let your power base slip. You worked too hard for it. How long will you be gone?"

"About a month, total. Two weeks in D.C., then a couple in Hawaii."

"Hawaii? Did I hear you right?"

"You heard me. Hines, did you know that whales migrate thousands of miles just to mate there?"

"Remarkable."

"I think so too. Merry Christmas, Hines."

"Same to you, sir."

As soon as Ben hung up, he reached into his desk drawer and pulled out Holly's gift. There would be no waffling this time. Before he could change his mind, he rushed to the hall closet and grabbed his blue jacket. Ramming her gift into his pocket, he hurried out the door.

Halfway to Holly's house he almost turned around and went back to the farm. She might be having a late lunch. Or an early dinner. She would have family there. Or she might be on the way to see her brother in Memphis.

Maybe she was taking a nap. After all, they had stayed up until the wee hours that morning.

The thought brought a smile to his lips. He patted his jacket pocket. He was absolutely going to give her the gift today.

The Snipeses were gone, Lily was napping, and a lemon icebox pie was sitting on the top shelf of the refrigerator. Holly cut a piece, kicked off her shoes, and settled into an easy chair. Maybe she didn't need it, but it was Christmas and she was tired and out of sorts. She deserved a small treat, and she was going to enjoy every morsel of it. After all, it was *her* pie.

Lily had not lost her touch. The pie was delicious down to the very last crumb. But somehow it had lost its magic. When she was a child, the mere sight of that paper-thin crust and that tall meringue was enough to make her feel good. Now it did nothing except make her feel stuffed.

Besides that, she was still cranky. She would blame it on the season if she didn't know better.

In her stockinged feet she padded to the kitchen, found a place for her plate in the crowded dishwasher, then turned it on. It was old and sounded like a freight train. She barely heard the doorbell over the racket.

"Coming," she said, hoping it wouldn't ring again and wake Lily.

Ben Sullivan was on her doorstep with the collar of his blue jacket turned up. She wanted to eat him up. Then she wanted to cry. Maybe her period was coming on and her hormones were raging.

"I hope I'm not disturbing you," he said.

Not in ways she wanted to talk about.

"You aren't," she said.

"I probably should have called first."

"That's all right. I'm having a quiet afternoon by myself."

"You're home alone?"

"Not alone. Lily's napping."

A door slammed across the street, and Holly could see Myrtle Maybry standing in her doorway gawking. By night everybody in the neighborhood would know that Holly had had a gentleman caller.

Except that sometimes Ben was no gentleman. She blushed to think it. Even now, with the way he was staring at her, he was definitely more rogue than gentleman. Holly figured she should have been absolutely delighted, but she wasn't. She was confused and slightly miffed, as if he had delivered a dozen long-stemmed red roses, then told her he'd made a mistake, that they were for someone in the house down the street.

"Did you have a good Christmas, Holly?"

He was so sincere and sweet that she almost forgave him, though what she had to forgive was mostly a mystery to her. Usually being female was an absolute pleasure, but sometimes being a woman was hard.

Sighing, Holly held open the door. "Forgive my lack of manners. Won't you come in?"

Oh, he was delicious looking in her den, just the right size to dominate the room without overpowering it, perfect for curling against on the sofa, with shoulders exactly right to rest her head and arms, designed for making her feel protected.

He sat on the sofa, leaving space for her to sit beside him, but she knew she'd be lost if she did. She chose a chair across the room from him, but the distance didn't help her distinguish between fantasy and reality. It did nothing to diminish her foolish, impossible dreams.

"Would you—"

"Have you—"

They both spoke at the same time, then looked at each other with such longing that it was impossible not to tell what they wanted: He wanted her, and she wanted him.

But to what degree and for how long? Those were the questions that haunted Holly.

"Ladies first," Ben said.

"Would you like some lemon icebox pie? My grandmother made it."

"It's tempting, but no thanks. I have packing to do and a plane to catch."

"You're leaving?"

Of course, he was. Every man she had ever cared about had left. Why should Ben Sullivan be any different?

"Yes." He pulled a plane ticket from his pocket. "And so are you, I hope."

She looked down at the ticket he handed her. *Holly Jones* it said. Destination, Hawaii.

"Merry Christmas, Holly."

"You bought this ticket for me?"

"Yes. I leave for D.C. early in the morning. In two weeks we'll meet in Atlanta and fly together from there."

"To Hawaii?"

"Didn't you say it was paradise? Didn't you tell me whales mated there?"

Not one word did he say about love or commitment. Not a single word did he utter about hope and plans for a future. Well, of course, whales mated there, but didn't they mate for life? Holly wasn't sure about that, but it seemed that the male whale was the kind of mammal who picked out one special female and hooked up with her for the rest of their days. And she would bet that not once did a male whale ever take his female counterpart for granted.

"I'm no whale," she said with asperity.

"I see," he said, but he didn't look as if he did. He looked puzzled.

Well, good for her. Good for him.

"You may think I'm the kind of woman who can be bought, just like you bought the Snipeses—"

"The Snipeses!" Ben was out of his seat, looking ready to explode. "How do you know about that?"

"This is a small town. It's impossible to keep a secret here."

He held her captive with his fierce regard. Holly began to waver. What if she was wrong about his motives? But wouldn't he say something to set her straight? Why didn't Ben *say* something?

"And you think I'm trying to buy you?" His voice was soft and deadly.

Suddenly Holly didn't know what to think. Reason was impossible with his eyes burning a hole in her.

"Keep the ticket, Holly. You've earned it."

He left so fast, she didn't have time to return the ticket to him.

"Wait," she said, but all the only response she got was the revving of the powerful Corvette's engine.

It was too late to call him back.

TWENTY

It was the first evening in the nearly two weeks since he had come to D.C. that Ben spent at home. His house in Georgetown was spacious, charming, and beautifully decorated. Some of his favorite antiques were there—the dining table and chairs he had found in a shop in Boston, an armoire he got in London, a rolltop desk from a little place off the coast of Maine.

His quiet house with its fine old furniture used to lift his spirits after a day of wheeling and dealing on Capitol Hill. But the magic was gone. Nothing had caught his interest since Holly. Nothing had lifted his spirits since Holly.

He put a frozen pot pie in the oven. It would be dinner. Though he had no appetite, he knew better than to go without food. Food was necessary for existence. A perfect word for his life. Existence. No spontaneous moments, no laughter, no passion, no unexpected encounters with a red-haired angel. Just getting from one day to the next.

That's what he had been doing ever since he left Mississippi. It was no way to live. Ben picked up the phone and called Hines.

"How are things in Mississippi?" he said.

"The same as when you called yesterday, sir."

Ordinarily Ben would have had a lively exchange with Hines about sarcasm, but even that small pleasure had lost its appeal.

"I was thinking, Hines. . . . There's no need for you to stay down there all by yourself. Why don't you hop on the next plane to D.C.?"

"Are you lonesome, sir?"

"I didn't say that." Ben cleared his throat. "How's Holly?"

Hines had become a regular at Holy Trinity since he'd returned from Virginia. "It gives me a reason to keep my shoes shined down here in the wilderness," was his explanation, but Ben suspected that Holly was the real reason for his transformation. She was like a magnet; everybody who knew her was drawn to her.

"Lively as ever, always smiling, always making people feel good."

"Do you think she misses me?"

"I would say so, sir."

"You would? Why?"

"Because every time I see her, she asks me the same question you do. 'How's Ben?' "

Ben felt a familiar rush of hope, but he quickly squelched it. He was not the kind of man women fell in love with, and no amount of effort could change that. He had been a fool ever to try.

"Don't tell her I asked about her, Hines."

"Certainly not, sir."

"Is she dating?"

"It's hardly likely a lady of her fine sensibilities is going to get over a broken heart in two weeks' time."

"You think her heart is broken?"

Ben didn't like to think of Holly suffering, but at the same time he was pleased that at least he had affected her to some degree.

"You might try calling her to ask."

"No. If a woman can't love me for what I am and accept what I have to offer, then I don't want her."

"It was just a suggestion, sir."

The acrid smell of burned food came from the direction of the kitchen.

"While I was wasting my time discussing a woman who wouldn't even go to Hawaii with me, my pot pie burned."

"Did you tell her you love her?"

"I told her that whales mated there."

"She's no whale."

"That's exactly what she said." A wisp of smoke curled around the corner of the kitchen door and drifted down the hallway. "I can't discuss this now, Hines, my house is burning down."

Ben stalked to the kitchen, grabbed a couple of pot holders, and jerked his pie from the oven. The fire alarm set up a raucous blaring. He opened the back door and fanned the smoke out with a dish towel.

"Love! Ha!" he said.

Love was nothing but a big pain in the ass. And to think he had tried to change his ways because of Holly Jones.

He was still fanning the smoke when his doorbell rang. Nobody ever came to call in D.C. It was probably one of the neighbors, arriving to say he had called the fire department.

"Coming," Ben yelled. "Just a minute."

He fanned vigorously until the smoke dispersed and the fire alarm ceased. Still clutching the dish towel, Ben stalked to the door.

And there stood Holly Jones, her hair glorious in the glow from the street lamps, her eyes as wide and innocent looking as he remembered, her mouth . . . Ben forced himself to stop devouring her with his eyes. He made himself remember that she didn't trust him, let alone love him.

"I probably should have called first," she said.

What would he have said if she had? Ben had no idea. All he knew was that Holly was on his doorstep and he still wanted her, still loved her—in spite of all that had happened.

The bad thing was, he still didn't know what to do about it. If anybody ever came up with a way to give lessons on love, he would make a fortune.

"This probably wasn't a good idea," she said, her eyes begging him to disagree.

But what if he did? She would come inside and he

would whisk her away to his bedroom and make mad passionate love to her. The way he felt they probably wouldn't even make it to the bedroom.

And then what? She had turned him down once. He didn't know if he could stand to fail with her again.

"I guess I should be going," she whispered.

His front porch was small, and she was across it in no time. She would be down the steps soon, then on the street hailing a cab that would take her to the airport, where she would fly back home and out of his life. This time forever.

A memory pierced him, a memory of Holly standing on his front porch in Mississippi saying practically the same thing she was saying now: "I shouldn't have come." Then later, inside his front room. What was it she had said? Something that almost broke his heart.

If only he could remember. She was halfway down the front steps now, and it was vitally important that he remember.

I don't want to be disposable.

Her words hit him with the force of a thunderbolt.

"Holly . . . wait."

She stopped. *Please turn around*, he silently pleaded.

"Don't go," he said.

When she turned he saw the tears glistening on her cheeks. How many ways would she break his heart? Could his heart be salvaged? Could hers?

She wavered, glancing toward the street then back at him.

"Please," he said. "I . . . need you, Holly."

Still she stood there. And he knew that if she left him, he would lose something that he could never recover: He would lose hope.

"I need you, too, Ben . . . but need is not enough."

She turned then, turned away and continued down the steps. Soon she would be on the sidewalk, and then at the curb. Down the street a cab came into view.

"Holly . . . I . . . let's talk."

"About what, Ben?"

"About you and me. About us."

"There is no *us*. You are in Washington and I'm in Tupelo. For a short while we came together and it was wonderful. At least for me it was. In the process I discovered something about myself: I discovered that I am worthy of more than being somebody's passing fancy. I am worthy of more than being somebody's fun-time party girl who will provide a few laughs in Birmingham and Hawaii."

"Is that what you thought, that I wanted to take you to Hawaii for a few laughs?"

"Didn't you?"

"No, that wasn't the reason."

"Then what was it, Ben? Tell me the reason."

There it was: the supreme test. Holly wanted to hear the words he couldn't say. Once he said them, he knew he could never take them back. He would be committed, for better or worse. He had seen the worst and it scared the hell out of him.

Her boots tapped on the bricks as she ran down the steps. "Taxi," she cried, lifting her hand.

The yellow cab pulled away from the corner and headed toward Ben's house. Fear of losing her lent him wings. He caught up with her on the sidewalk. With both hands on her shoulders, he turned her around.

"Don't go, Holly."

"Why?"

"Because . . . I love you."

Ben felt a wave of relief. Saying the words hadn't been as hard as he imagined.

"I love you, Holly," he said once more, and then he laughed for sheer joy. "Hines should be here to see this. I feel like dancing in the streets. . . . Maybe I will."

It was twenty degrees, and he wasn't even wearing a coat, but Ben never felt the chill. He spun her around on the sidewalk, and when the cab pulled up beside the curb, Ben handed the drive a twenty-dollar bill.

"For your trouble," he said. "The lady won't be needing you."

"Thanks, mister. And whatever it is you and the pretty lady are dancing about, congratulations."

"The pretty lady and I are getting married."

"Hey, congratulations again. When's the big day?"

Holly laughed. "He has no idea. Besides, I haven't even said yes yet."

"Looks to me like that's not going to be a problem," the cabbie said. "So long, y'all. Many happy returns."

He waved at them as he drove off.

"Would you say that accent is from Georgia or Mississippi?" Ben said.

"South Carolina," Holly said.

"How could you tell?"

"By the way he pronounced his *r*'s. . . . Are you going to invite me in? I'd like to hear more about this wedding you're planning."

Inside, they stopped briefly in the hallway to hang up her coat. There was much he needed to say, much he needed to hear her say, but at the moment he had a more pressing need.

His bed was brass with a thick comforter that was exactly right for the wild passionate reunion they had. And when it was over, he held her close.

"I can't believe I almost lost you," he said.

"I was so afraid of loving you."

"Why?"

"Because I didn't think you could love *me*. It was not until after you left that I began to realize that any time we love, we take a risk. And then I knew that I had to come to you, no matter what happened. I love you and have almost from the first time I laid eyes on you. I had to let you know that, because you are worth the risk, Ben."

"And so I loaded Lily up in the car and drove to

Memphis and said, 'I'll be back in a few weeks, James.'" Smiling, she rested her forehead against his. "Loving you has made a bold woman of me."

"You didn't need me for that. You were always a bold woman."

His blood began to stir again, and he knew it would always be that way with this woman. When he entered her, she wrapped her arms around him and pulled him close.

"There's something I have to know, Benjamin G. Sullivan the Third."

"Now?"

"Yes, now. What does the G stand for?"

"Gabriel."

"The angel!"

"Hardly," he said. And then he proved her wrong.

EPILOGUE

The Fellowship Hall at Holy Trinity was decorated with hanging greens, wreaths of holly, and bright red bows. A pile of fresh straw in the west corner served as a makeshift stable.

This year, though, the animals were docile and extremely well behaved. They were enormous cardboard cutouts fashioned painstakingly by Hines, who stood watch over them dressed in the garb of a shepherd. He had made the headpiece from a towel, but the robe was compliments of Loweva.

"I've never seen you look better, Hines," Ben said, grinning. "You should wear pink terry cloth more often."

"Pay him no attention, Hines," Holly said. "He's just jealous. At least yours covers your knees."

"Those are nice knees you have there, sir."

Ben, who was playing the part of Joseph, stood on

the stage beside his wife, who looked angelic in her role of Mary. Holly's blue bathrobe didn't even cover his knees.

"Of course, Joseph wasn't six-four," she had told him that morning before they left the farmhouse.

Over the intercom came the joyful sounds of "O Little Town of Bethlehem." The church was packed to the rafters, and soon the crowd would spill over into the Fellowship Hall for doughnuts and coffee. But mostly for a good look at this year's Christmas Nativity. After the previous year's show, no one dared miss it.

"Early church is almost over," Holly said.

"Time for the show." With a grin as big as Texas, Ben looked down at the baby in his arms. "Are you ready for the show, big boy?"

For a moment the baby regarded him solemnly with wide blue eyes, then he cooed and blew a spit bubble.

"Did you hear that? I think he said Daddy."

Holly patted his arm. "Three-month-old babies can't talk, darling. You're just prejudiced."

"You heard him, didn't you, Hines?"

"Indeed, I did, sir. He's a regular genius."

"Remind me to give you a nice increase in your Christmas bonus."

"I already took care of that, sir."

The door burst open as the first of the early-churchgoers poured in.

Holly adjusted the tiny halo on her son's flaming

red hair, and Ben carefully placed him on a soft cush-
ion in the manger.

"He looks like an angel," Holly said softly.

"Why should that surprise you?" Ben squeezed
his wife's hand. "I seem to have a knack for finding
angels."

THE EDITORS' CORNER

What better way to celebrate the holidays than with four sensual and exciting new LOVESWEPTs. Whether they're searching for treasure or battling bad guys, our heroes are sure to deliver thrills, laughs, and passion as they do whatever they must to win the hearts of our heroines. So curl up in your favorite chair with a blanket and a cup of hot cocoa and enjoy!

Starting off our fabulous lineup is Marcia Evanick with **TANGLED UP IN BLUE**, LOVESWEPT #818. He's expecting a gray-haired housesitter who plays bingo when she isn't baking cookies or dusting, but when Matt Stone returns unannounced, he discovers instead a golden-haired nymph splashing naked in his pool! Beulah Crawford, nicknamed Blue, is the picture of sweet chaos, a delightful scamp who revels in living for the moment. Now all Matt has to do is make her believe that family isn't just an impossible dream. Hailed by *Romantic Times* for "delighting readers with her marvelous blend of love and laughter," Marcia Evanick won't let readers down in this funny tale of cat and mouse romance.

Watch out, villains! Cynthia Powell has found a **HERO FOR HIRE**, LOVESWEPT #819. Cade Jackson has a face too hard to be handsome, Martinique Duval decides, and a smile just lethal enough to make a good girl want to be bad! Tracking his quarry has led the tough bounty hunter straight to this wildfire angel, but keeping her safe means risking a heart he didn't know he had. Can her innocence give a reluctant hero with a scarred soul a reason to stop running forever? Rising star Cynthia Powell proves once again that every man is susceptible to the call of true love.

Talented newcomer Eve Gaddy believes that two people in love can never be **TOO CLOSE FOR COMFORT**, LOVESWEPT #820. Jack Corelli vows to keep Marissa Fairfax alive to testify, but guarding the cool trauma surgeon means long, hot hours in close quarters with a woman who challenges him to break all of his rules! She barely trembles when held at gunpoint, but Jack's slow, sizzling attack on her mouth makes her shiver and burn. Together, this wounded hero and the lady he'd die to protect must learn to silence ghosts and survive a desperate betrayal. Eve Gaddy takes readers on a heart-palpitating ride as she weaves a tale you won't soon forget!

When you're gambling with love, everything is **UP FOR GRABS**, LOVESWEPT #821, by Kristen Robinette. Jesse McCain steps onto her land without asking, a bold buccaneer who knows the stormy-eyed lady won't deny him a chance to dig up her property—and her past! Targeted by a grin full of promises, Lauren Adams feels her resistance melt, but the brash archeologist isn't telling her all he knows. Still, she isn't one to back down from a challenge, so she follows Jesse down an unknown path and ends up losing her heart to a road warrior with a secret. In a debut that readers are sure to enjoy, Kristen delivers a top-notch romance full of tenderness and passion.

Happy reading!

With warmest wishes,

Beth de Guzman

Shauna Summers

Beth de Guzman   Shauna Summers

Senior Editor   Editor

P.S. Watch for these Bantam women's fiction titles coming in January: From Sandra Brown, the author of twenty-nine *New York Times* bestselling titles, comes **HAWK O'TOOLE'S HOSTAGE**, a riveting contemporary romance in which a woman is held hostage by a desperate man . . . and a desperate desire. Now available in paperback, **THE UGLY DUCKLING** is a thrilling novel of contemporary suspense by *New York Times* bestselling author Iris Johansen. From Susan Johnson, mistress of erotic romance, comes **WICKED**, a spectacular romance of suspense and seduction. And finally, **HEART OF THE FALCON** by Suzanne Robinson captures the passion of Egypt as a defiant beauty fights to regain her birthright. Don't miss the previews of these exceptional novels in next month's LOVESWEPTs. And immediately following this page, sneak a peek at the Bantam women's fiction titles on sale *now*!

For current information on Bantam's women's fiction, visit our new web site, *Isn't It Romantic*, at the following address: **http://www.bdd.com/romance**

Don't miss these extraordinary books
by your favorite Bantam authors

On sale in November:

AFTER CAROLINE
by Kay Hooper

BREAKFAST IN BED
by Sandra Brown

DON'T TALK TO STRANGERS
by Bethany Campbell

LORD SAVAGE
by Patricia Coughlin

LOVE'S A STAGE
by Sharon and Tom Curtis

from

Kay Hooper

Her sensuous and evocative voice has made her a
nationally bestselling author, and now she weaves a
haunting new tale of contemporary suspense, a
gripping emotional tapestry of two women bound
together in the desperation of one fatal moment—
and the urgent need to uncover the truth.

AFTER CAROLINE

Joanna Flynn was lucky to be alive. Twice in a matter
of minutes she almost died on a patch of oil-slicked
highway. But when the doctors told her that she
would suffer no lasting effects, they were wrong. For
that night the dreams began. . . .

They were of a house perched high above the sea,
of a ticking clock, and the lingering scent of roses. Yet
night after night Joanna awoke with a sense of panic.
Terror lingered throughout her days, urging her to do
something—but what? Then two strangers on the
street called her Caroline, and Joanna knew she had
to find an explanation for what was happening, or
she'd lose her mind.

What she finally uncovered was an obituary for a
woman named Caroline McKenna—a woman who
looked enough like her to be her twin, a woman who
was killed in a car accident on the same day Joanna
should have perished. Now her torturous nightmares
and a tenuous connection have brought Joanna three
thousand miles across country to the town where
Caroline lived—and died. Almost everyone has stories

to tell about Cliffside's leading lady, and yet no one seems to have known her. Was she the shy wife or the seductress of men? The devoted mother or the selfish beauty?

Too soon Joanna realizes that it's not her sanity at stake, but her life. For unraveling the mystery of Caroline means uncovering the secrets in this picturesque town, secrets someone may have killed to hide. And that someone appears all too willing to kill again.

AVAILABLE IN HARDCOVER

Sandra Brown

Her novels are sensual and moving, compelling and richly satisfying. Now the *New York Times* bestselling author of *Heaven's Price* captures the wrenching dilemma of a woman tempted by an unexpected—and forbidden—love. . . .

BREAKFAST IN BED

Hurt one too many times in the past, Sloan Fairchild is convinced that she will never be able to trust her heart to a man again. Instead, she pours all her energy into making a success of her elegant San Francisco bed-and-breakfast inn. But when her best friend asks her to house her fiancé for a month, Sloan opens the doors of Fairchild House to Carter Madison . . . and meets a man who turns her world—and her concept of herself—upside down.

Carter, a bestselling author, is looking for a little peace and quiet so he can finish his latest novel before his wedding. The last thing he expects is to find himself instantly attracted to his hostess—or her to him. As the days pass, Sloan tries to ignore the feelings this handsome, disturbingly perceptive man stirs in her . . . tries to stop herself from dreaming dreams that can never be. But as Carter reveals his overwhelming desire for her, Sloan is left to struggle against her own deepest longing: to know just once how it feels to be truly cherished.

Caught between love and loyalty to her best friend, Sloan must search her soul and make a choice: to love for the moment, walk away forever, or fight to have it all.

AVAILABLE IN PAPERBACK

A seductive game of hide-and-seek

Bethany Campbell

Nationally bestselling author of *See How They Run*

DON'T TALK TO STRANGERS

One by one the women were disappearing. Each had been young, vulnerable . . . and spending time "chatting" on the Internet with a mysterious stranger. It was Carrie Blue's job to track down that stranger, to put herself on the Internet in the guise of a lonely young student and smoke out a cunningly seductive killer. But soon she is drawn inexorably into a world where truth is indistinguishable from fiction . . . and it proves far more difficult than she could have imagined to resist the lure of a twisted mind—one that may already have figured out who Carrie is, and marked her as his next kill. . . .

"Carrie, look at me."

She struggled to keep control of her voice. "No."

"Yes," he said. "Are you afraid to? Why?"

She let her hands drop to her lap, straightened, and gave him a resentful glance. But she couldn't hold his gaze, and looked at the window instead, where the rain blurred the glass to a gray translucence.

"I know you were in the pub last night, alone," he said. "Then the Highwayman came in. You broke your connection, and he logged off immediately after. He never came back."

"How do you know all this?"

"I've learned a few tricks. I can see you from a

distance. Where you are and who you're with. But not what you're doing."

"You learned to do that from reading the archives?"

"Yes."

"You spy on me?"

"I monitor you and Brooke. Every fifteen minutes."

Carrie shrugged and said nothing.

"So what happened with the Highwayman?" he asked again.

"That's my business."

"It's my business too. There's a girl in a morgue in Illinois. Doesn't that matter?"

Her cheeks went hot and she shot him a glance of rebuke. "Of course it matters."

"So what about this Highwayman? What in God's name went on between you?"

Oh, hell, she thought wearily. If Hayden wanted the truth so much, she'd give it to him, right between the eyes. She no longer gave a damn about her pride, and it was Hayden who'd led her into this nasty farce.

"He was drunk. He wanted netsex. I said I wouldn't, not with someone who wouldn't tell me his name. So I broke the connection."

"I tried your private line," Hayden said. "It was busy. He phoned you?"

Carrie took a deep breath and told him what Paul Johnson had said. "I believe him. It makes me feel sick. This poor, disabled kid in love with a girl who doesn't exist. I want to hang myself."

Her chin trembled, and she thought, *I will not cry again. I will not let him see me cry. No one has seen me cry for ten years.*

Hayden's expression grew guarded. He might have been surprised or repelled, but all he said was "Carrie, Monica Toussant and Gretchen Small believed somebody too. What if it's not true? It's a damn good story. He loves you, and only you can heal him."

Carrie resisted the desire to pick up the coffee mug and fling it at his head. "If he's lying, he's contemptible. If he isn't, I'm contemptible. And if he's telling the truth, I couldn't stand it. The very thought makes me feel slimy."

He frowned. "He says his name's Paul Johnson? And he's not a citizen of the U.S.? How many guys do you suppose are named Paul Johnson in North America? He's got your phone number, but do you have his?"

"No," Carrie said. "So what?"

"He's living with a married sister, but you don't know her last name?"

She tilted her chin to a rebellious angle. "No."

"So how do you trace him, Carrie? How do you know he's for real? Do you have his address?"

"No," she said. "Stop trying to change my mind."

"I've got to. What if he's not some poor, disabled kid who thinks he's in love with you? What if he's an excellent liar who's stalking you?"

"What if he's not?" she challenged. "What if he's a twenty-three-year-old man who may never walk again? What then?"

"If we find out that's true, you let him down easy. It's not as if the two of you really know each other."

"He wants to have netsex with me, for God's sake. And I've encouraged him. I've let him hold me in his arms, hug me, kiss me."

He searched her face for a moment. Her confused emotions grew more tumultuous. *Something's going to happen,* she thought. *And I haven't got the strength to stop it.*

He said, "He's never touched you."

He put his hand to her face, his fingertips grazing first her cheekbone, then her jawline. With thumb and forefinger he lightly cupped her chin. "This is touching."

Her heart thudded crazily. She told herself, *Don't let this happen.*

"And he hasn't really kissed you," he breathed.

He tipped her face to his and brought his mouth to bear on hers, gently at first, then more hungrily.

Oh, God, oh, God, oh, God, she thought, her heart leaping.

He's real. He's real.

She had eight weeks to tame a savage—
and to fall in love.

LORD SAVAGE

by

Patricia Coughlin

*The request was impossible. Unthinkable. And unavoidable.
Ariel Halliday couldn't refuse the head of the Penrose School
when he asked her to take on the particularly difficult as-
signment—not if she wanted to stay in his good graces. Now
she has only eight weeks to transform a savage raised on a
distant Pacific island into a gentleman. Yet nothing could
prepare her for the darkly handsome "pupil" who is the heir
apparent of the Marquis of Sage.*

Ariel stepped inside the room and heard the door shut
behind her with a click that sounded as irrevocable as a
gunshot. She closed her eyes briefly, caught her breath,
and took a determined step forward.

"Good afternoon," she said. Another breath. In.
Out. She could do this. "I'm Miss Halliday. Miss Ariel
Halliday. I know that you're Leon Nicholas Duvanne,
the fifth Marquis of Sage. I'm just not sure that you
know it yet," she added ruefully.

She set the tray on the small table a few feet from
his cot.

"Of course you have a whole mouthful of other
titles I shall not even attempt to recite for you now. I
believe Lord Sav—Sage will suit nicely for the time
being."

Ninny, she thought. Such a slip of the tongue
might have made for a most uneasy moment. That is, if
he even understood a word she was saying. There was
still no indication he did. For that matter, there was no

obvious sign the man was alive, but for the slow, steady rise and fall of his very imposing chest.

Ariel, trying not to stare in fascination at the wedge of silky dark chest hair, wet her suddenly dry lips with her tongue.

"Proper manners," she began, "dictate that a gentleman rise when a lady enters the room and greet her by title and name. I am prepared to overlook your failure to do so on this occasion, overtaxed as I'm sure you must be from your obviously high level of exertion thus far today." He offered no response to her sarcasm.

"I do believe, however," she continued, "that in consideration of the fact that I have gone to considerable trouble to bring you tea, you could at the very least turn your head and acknowledge that I am speaking to you."

To her amazement, the dark head began to slowly turn her way. He understood, she thought excitedly. Either her words or her chilly tone, she couldn't be certain which, but he had clearly understood something. And he had responded.

Her excitement turned to apprehension as he proceeded to swing his feet to the floor and stand, facing her fully. She fought an urge to step back. He made no move to come closer, however, and her heartbeat gradually slowed to as near normal as she expected it to be while she remained confined there alone with him.

His gaze caught and held hers and Ariel found that the effect of his silent presence was even more daunting when he was staring directly into her eyes. He was, she concluded, without question the most beautiful man she had ever seen. Never before had she thought to describe a man as beautiful, but the word came to her easily and naturally when she gazed at Lord Sage's serene face and strong, lean body. He appeared to her as masculine perfection, chiseled by the hand of the greatest master of all.

His cheekbones were aristocratically high, his jaw

beneath the short black beard classically square, his mouth full, with just enough of a slant to add interest to his otherwise perfect face. A stray lock of his long, raven hair hung loosely across his forehead, and his eyes, deep-set and almond-shaped, were a quite extraordinary shade. Brown velvet swirled with gold, dark and bright at once, like sunlight on ancient brass. Tiger's eyes, Ariel mused, thinking of the gemstone by that name. Hard and gleaming and exotic.

At that moment the expression in his remarkable eyes was nether warm nor cold, neither friendly nor antagonistic. It was shuttered. She felt certain that the man was no dolt, and that although he would not permit her to be privy to it, there was a great deal of thought and evaluation going on inside his head. In fact, some instinct warned her that his lordship was taking her measure just as calculatedly as she was taking his.

She straightened, smoothing a few stray wisps of light brown hair. Why hadn't she taken more pains in arranging the chignon at the back of her neck that morning? she lamented. And perhaps worn a newer dress? One in a more flattering color? She quickly marshaled her thoughts, reminding herself that she did not possess a newer dress and that gray was a most serviceable hue for everyday wear and besides that, it mattered not at all what the man before her thought of her appearance.

Without warning he shook back his hair, dislodging the lock that hung over his forehead to reveal a two-inch-long scar there. The imperfection, which would have marred the appeal of most men, enhanced his instead. For the first time Ariel noticed the array of other small marks and scars that covered his body, souvenirs, it seemed to her, of a life far more reckless and exciting than her own. Feeling a mixture of curiosity and envy, she lifted her gaze to his to find him watching her with his eyes narrowed in suspicion.

The eagerly awaited reissue of a memorable classic
by

Sharon and Tom Curtis

LOVE'S A STAGE

Frances Atherton came to London to explore the plot that sent her father to prison. But she never imagined that she, too, would be held captive—by the charms of London's most scandalous playwright and fascinating rake. Devastatingly handsome Lord David Landry has charmed any number of women, and makes it clear that Frances is next. . . .

He had said there were two reasons he had been following her on Charles Street, the first being that he was concerned about her safely reaching her destination. It was true, Frances thought, that she might have had a difficult time locating her great-aunt's new address without him.

"But what was the second?"

"I beg your pardon?" he said, sending his sweet smiling glance at her.

"The second reason you followed me."

He looked, if not precisely surprised, then a little curious; he studied her face as if to revise a prior impression. His eyes were bright and kind as he said, "Miss Atherton, surely you must know."

The wind's mischievous fingers had loosened her bonnet strings. She retied them rapidly as she walked.

"Well, I don't. And as we've been walking along, it occurs to me to wonder why you would want to spend your time helping strangers around the streets, because I can see now, even if I did not at first, that you are quite a brilliant man."

It was his turn to be amused. "*Thank* you, Miss Atherton. You honor me too much. Do you know, though, that if you continue in that vein, I will find myself revising my previous estimate on the size of your hamlet downward. Hasn't anyone ever tried to seduce you?"

Seduce. She knew the word, of course, but it had previously played so minute a part in her vocabulary that she was forced to think a moment to recall its meaning. She gasped when she remembered and said simply, "No."

"That's quite an oversight on somebody's part." A crowded street corner was not the setting a man of his vast experience would have chosen to make a declaration of desire, nor was a bald statement of fact as likely to produce a successful result as were patience and attentive intimacy. To have ignored her direct appeal for an explanation, though, would have amounted to a deception alien to his nature.

A grin touched his lips as he noted they had arrived almost at the ornamental porch that marked the entrance to Miss Isles's apartments—at least, when she demanded the return of her case, she would have only a short space to carry it. "Miss Atherton," he said gently, "I would like to be more than friends with you."

Frances's young life had been devoted to duty and service. She was assistant mother to eight younger siblings, confidante and soul mate to her papa and aide-de-camp to her unworldly, domestically inclined mama. Excepting her brothers, the only young men Frances knew were the fishermen's sons from her village, any one of whom would have been too shy to woo the parson's lovely, intelligent daughter. There had been no proposals, proper or improper, in Miss Atherton's life, and while she might daydream in modesty of the former, it had never crossed her mind that she might ever be in a position to receive the latter. So unexpected was the declaration that Miss Atherton was not completely sure of his intention until he said helpfully, "Yes, Miss Atherton, I meant precisely what you think I meant."

To say that Frances was shocked would have been greatly to understate the case; in fact, she was astonished. She had never been encouraged to think of herself as pretty. As a result, she did not, and it came as a surprise to her that she could somehow have inspired those sentiments in any gentleman, particularly one who, it was quite obvious, could hardly have suffered from a lack of feminine companionship. Her incredulous surprise, however, was soon trampled by a flaming wrath.

"I suppose you think," she said dangerously, "that because I *allowed* you to talk to me on the street you can insult me!"

Capped in her shabby brown bonnet and cloaked in her puritanical morality, she had for him the quaint charm of a delightfully apt cliché. They had reached Miss Isles's building, so he set her case on the low porch before the door and took Miss Atherton's flushed cheeks leisurely between his palms, forcing her to look into his sparkling green eyes.

"Never, Prudence," he said with what Frances regarded as an odious tranquillity, "is it an insult to tell a woman that you find her so attractive that you would like to—"

Miss Atherton stopped his words by clapping her mittened hands over her ears in a gesture rendered unfortunately inefficient by the oversized contours of her bonnet. She removed her face from his hold with so forceful a back-step that if it were not for his steadying hands on her shoulders, she would surely have fallen.

"It is always, *al-ways*," she said furiously, "an insult unless preceded by a marriage vow."

Releasing her shoulders, he walked to the heavy

oak door and held it open for her. Miss Atherton marched past and found they had entered a narrow hall lined with marble wallpaper in yellow and brown. An interior door lay to the right of the entrance, and a wooden open-newel stair lit by a single lamp led to an upper landing. He lifted her case inside the threshold and shut the outer door behind them.

There was both rueful self-knowledge and compassion in his smile as he said, "That's one game I don't play, Prudence. I doubt if I'll ever be able to make that type of commitment to a woman. Honestly, sweetheart, there's very little chance I'd marry you."

Miss Atherton came to a full rolling boil. "Well, there is *no* chance that I would marry you!" She stormed to the door like a tidal wave and pounded against it with her fist.

On sale in December:

HAWK O'TOOLE'S HOSTAGE
by Sandra Brown

THE UGLY DUCKLING
by Iris Johansen

WICKED
by Susan Johnson

HEART OF THE FALCON
by Suzanne Robinson

DON'T MISS THESE FABULOUS
BANTAM WOMEN'S FICTION TITLES

On Sale in December

HAWK O'TOOLE'S HOSTAGE
by *New York Times* megaselling phenomenon SANDRA BROWN
Another heady blend of the passion, humor, and high-voltage romantic suspense that has made Sandra Brown one of the most beloved writers in America. Now in hardcover for the first time, this is the thrilling tale of a woman who finds herself at the mercy of a handsome stranger—and the treacherous feelings only he can arouse. ____ 10448-9 $17.95/$24.95

"A spectacular tale of revenge, betrayal and survival." —*Publishers Weekly*
From *New York Times* bestselling author IRIS JOHANSEN comes

THE UGLY DUCKLING in paperback ____ 56991-0 $5.99/$7.99

"Susan Johnson is queen of erotic romance." —*Romantic Times*

WICKED
by bestselling author SUSAN JOHNSON
No one sizzles like Susan Johnson, and she burns up the pages in *Wicked*. Governess Serena Blythe had been saving for years to escape to Florence. Despite her well-laid plans, there were two developments she couldn't foresee: that she would end up a stowaway—and that the ship's master would be an expert at seduction. ____ 57214-8 $5.99/$7.99

From the bestselling author of *The Engagement* SUZANNE ROBINSON

HEART OF THE FALCON
Rich with the pageantry of ancient Egypt and aflame with the unforgettable romance of a woman who has lost everything only to find the man who will brand her soul, this is the unforgettable Suzanne Robinson at her finest. ____ 28138-0 $5.50/$7.50

Ask for these books at your local bookstore or use this page to order.

Please send me the books I have checked above. I am enclosing $____ (add $2.50 to cover postage and handling). Send check or money order, no cash or C.O.D.'s, please.

Name _____

Address _____

City/State/Zip _____

Send order to: Bantam Books, Dept. FN158, 2451 S. Wolf Rd., Des Plaines, IL 60018
Allow four to six weeks for delivery.
Prices and availability subject to change without notice.   FN 158 12/96